"I can't stop thinking about you."

The damning words just sort of popped out, and Megan couldn't regret saying them.

Greg asked, "And is that such a bad thing?"

"No." She traced the handle of her mug with a finger. "Yes. Oh, I don't know."

He chuckled. "Well, at least that's one thing you're sure about."

"You think this is funny?" she chided. "Because it's not—not in the least."

"I know." His voice was soft and low. Intimate. Tender. "I've been thinking…."

She had to swallow before she could speak. "About?"

"You."

Dear Reader,

Don't you just love it when the nice girl finishes first? I do.

Take Megan Schumacher, She's about the nicest woman on Danbury Way. All the women of the neighborhood like Megan. Everyone *trusts* her. They tell her their secrets. They cry on her shoulder when things go wrong.

But the real truth is, Megan, like most of the women of Danbury Way, has a few secrets of her own. Like that crush she had on sweet Carly Alderson's ex, Greg Banning. Now, there's a secret that will never be revealed. Because Greg's a total hunk and would never in a million years be interested in nondescript Megan.

Or would he? *Mwahaha.*

Welcome to Danbury Way, where everybody knows everybody's business—and talks about it. A lot.

Best always,

Christine Rimmer

CHRISTINE RIMMER

THE RELUCTANT CINDERELLA

Silhouette

SPECIAL EDITION

Published by Silhouette Books

America's Publisher of Contemporary Romance

Special thanks and acknowledgment are given to
Christine Rimmer for her contribution to the
TALK OF THE NEIGHBORHOOD miniseries.

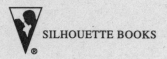 SILHOUETTE BOOKS

RECYCLED PAPER · RECYCLED PAPER

ISBN-13: 978-0-373-24765-3
ISBN-10:   0-373-24765-6

THE RELUCTANT CINDERELLA

Visit Silhouette Books at www.eHarlequin.com

Printed in U.S.A.

CHRISTINE RIMMER

came to her profession the long way around. Before settling down to write about the magic of romance, she'd been everything from an actress to a salesclerk to a waitress. Now that she's finally found work that suits her perfectly, she insists she never had a problem keeping a job—she was merely gaining "life experience" for her future as a novelist. Christine is grateful not only for the joy she finds in writing, but for what waits when the day's work is through: a man she loves, who loves her right back, and the privilege of watching their children grow and change day to day. She lives with her family in Oklahoma. Visit Christine at her new home on the Web at www.christinerimmer.com.

For my fellow authors on this project.
As always, it was a joy working with you.

Chapter One

"Aunt Megan, I really, *really* need to go," Olivia whispered anxiously.

Bent over to child level as she dumped the dishwasher detergent in the tray, Megan Schumacher snapped the tray shut, straightened to push the start button and shoved the door into lock position. Inside, the whooshing started. She edged the box of detergent onto the crowded kitchen counter and turned to look fondly down at her niece.

"Powder room." Megan pointed the way. "Quick."

Blond curls bounced as the little sweetie shook her head. "Someone's in there." She wrinkled her button nose in childish disgust. "Being sick. And there's someone upstairs in *our* bathroom, too." She meant the bathroom she shared with her brothers, Anthony and Michael. "Crying."

Great. "What about your mom's bathr—"

Olivia cut her off with a snort of wounded frustration. "Anthony's in there. He *yelled* at me to go away."

Anthony, the oldest of Megan's sister's kids, was nine. He'd developed a bit of an attitude lately. If he wasn't silent and sulky, he was ordering everyone to leave him alone.

Olivia rolled her blue eyes. "Aunt Megan. Come *on*. I need to use *your* bathroom."

"Well, sure. Why didn't you just say so?"

Olivia let out a pained sigh. "Is it *open?*"

"You bet. Need help?"

The little girl drew herself up and spoke with great dignity. "Thank you. No. After all, I *am* seven." Then she whirled and took off for the kitchen door that led to the breezeway and the backyard entrance to Megan's apartment over the garage.

"She's a cutie, that one." Marti Vincente, who lived next door, pulled a tray of stuffed miniature portobello mushrooms from the oven. The neighbors took turns hosting the annual Danbury Way early summer block party, but Marti and her husband always provided most of the food. The stuffed mushrooms looked as delicious as everything else Marti and Ed had brought over to Angela's bright kitchen that day.

Slim, stylish and attractive, Marti worked full-time at the restaurant she and Ed owned. She was up close and personal with all that wonderful food on a daily basis—and she couldn't weigh more than one-ten. How fair was that?

Megan looked down at her own baggy orange T-shirt and frayed jeans. Beneath the comfortable old clothes, she was no Marti Vincente. And she probably never would be.

"Mushroom?" Marti offered. "I've got some that are slightly cooled right here...."

Megan needed no more urging. She popped one of the delicious morsels into her mouth and groaned in delight. "Incredible." Through the window over the sink, she could see the neighbors gathered in groups under the shade of the patio cover, chatting and laughing, sipping iced drinks and chowing down on the Vincentes' delicious finger food.

Angela was out there, too, weaving in and out among her guests, carrying a trayful of Vincente delicacies. Since her sister was busy, that left Megan to check on Olivia's story of sickness and sobbing in the bathrooms. Resigned, Megan swallowed the last of that to-die-for mushroom, thanked Marti and headed off down the back hall.

She found Rebecca Peters hovering by the door to the powder room.

Rebecca was subletting the house on the other side of the Vincentes. She wore a skinny, strappy sundress in her trademark black, with the usual four-inch designer heels to match. Rebecca was *so* not the suburban type. No one in the neighborhood could understand why she'd moved to Rosewood, which was an hour-and-a-half train ride north of New York City and about as suburban as any town could get.

Her worried frown had Megan asking, "What's up?"

Rebecca's frown deepened. "I think Molly's in there...."

Molly owned the house at 7 Danbury Way. Happily single, she put most of her energy into her mega-successful consulting firm.

"Is she sick?" Megan asked softly.

Rebecca nodded and pitched her voice to a confidential level. "She was fine. We were chatting out on the patio. And then she got this strange, green look and..." Rebecca shook her sleek brown head. "I don't know. I just don't know..."

Megan took charge, moving in close, tapping lightly on the door, asking gently, "Molly? Molly, are you all right?"

Several seconds passed before she answered, "Fine." Her voice was bright and cheerful—too much so. "Be right out." She practically sang the words. A moment later, the door swung inward and Molly emerged on a suspicious cloud of minty-fresh scent: breath spray. No doubt about it. "Hey." Molly fluffed her long, curly hair and smiled a wide, forced smile. "Great party, huh? Megan, I don't know how that sister of yours does it. Single with three kids and a full-time job. But the house looks fabulous and the party is...perfect." She patted Megan's arm. "I'm sure it helps to have you here to pitch in."

Before Megan could reply, Rebecca tried again. "Molly, are you certain you're—"

Molly didn't even let her finish. "Whew. I need some of that lemonade Angela's been passing around. How 'bout you?"

Rebecca got the message: whatever had been going on behind the powder room door, Molly had no intention of discussing it. "Uh. Well, alrighty. Sounds great. Megan?"

Megan still had to make sure the crier upstairs in the kids' bathroom was all right. And check on Anthony. "You guys go ahead."

So the two women turned and left her just as Zooey Finnegan, the gorgeous model-slim, auburn-haired nanny who looked after widower Jack Lever's kids, came through the arch from the family room. "Terrific party," she said with a warm smile as she slipped into the empty powder room and softly shut the door.

Megan made for the stairs. Halfway up, she ran into Anthony, who came barreling down paying zero attention to where he was going.

"Whoa, there, cowboy." Megan laughed, catching him by the arms and righting him before he fell against the stair rail.

"Sorry, Aunt Megan," he muttered, looking down.

"No prob." She waited until he slanted her a glance before softly chiding, "Olivia says you yelled at her."

He let out a snort. "Well, I was in the *bathroom*. She kept knocking. What'd she expect?"

"She didn't expect yelling," Megan said quietly. "Yelling is not a good thing."

"Okay, okay." He stuck out his lower lip, but he did mutter, "I'm sorry."

"Tell that to your sister."

He was staring at his shoes again. "Awright, I will. Can I go now? Please?"

She released him. "Remember. No running on the—"

He'd already zipped around her and was headed down—fast, but no longer at a run. He called over his shoulder, "Okay, okay. I won't. I promise."

Megan stared after him for a second or two, smiling a doting auntie's smile. Anthony was a good kid. He'd get past this sulky phase—soon, she hoped.

And there was still the crier in the kids' bath to see about.

In the upstairs hall, the door to the bathroom was shut. Megan stood in front of it and wondered what she should do next. She couldn't hear any crying coming from in there. Maybe she should just—

Wait. There: a sob. A stifled one, but still. A definite sob.

So, okay. Maybe a little further investigation was required. She waited—and yep. There it was again: another sob, followed by a distinct sniffle and a tiny, choked-off wail. Olivia had got it right. Someone was in there crying.

When you cried in the bathroom at a block party, well, you should get sympathy. Someone should come and lend a shoulder to cry on.

That would be Megan. On Danbury Way, where she'd lived for three years now, Megan was considered a person everybody could trust: nonthreatening, patient and understanding. All the women liked her. They could tell her anything and she'd never betray their secrets.

Sometimes the role of confidante got a little old, especially lately, when so much had changed in her life outside the neighborhood. But then again, somebody had to "be there" for everyone else. And Megan was used to it. She'd been fitting in, getting along and listening to everybody else's problems, since she was seven and a half years old.

Discreetly, she tapped on the bathroom door.

Silence.

After a thirty-second interval, she tapped again.

More silence.

Finally, she spoke. "It's Megan. Are you...all right in there?"

Another silence. Then a sniffle. And finally, hopefully, a woman murmured, "Megan?" More sniffling. "Is it really..." A sob. A tiny hiccup, then, "...you?" Even with all the sniffling, Megan recognized that soft Texas drawl. It was Carly Alderson.

Megan probably should have known. She made her voice even gentler. "Come on, Carly. Let me in...."

A second later, the door opened. Carly, strikingly pretty even with puffy eyes and a red nose, sniffled, sobbed and ushered Megan inside. Once Megan stood on the fluffy green bathroom rug with her, Carly shut the door and punched the lock.

Then, with a mournful little groan, she sank to the edge of the tub. Megan got the box of tissues from the sink counter and sat down beside her.

"Oh, Megan…" Carly paused to sniffle some more. She wiped her nose with a torn-up, wrinkled bit of tissue. "I just…I can't…"

"Here." Megan extended the box.

Carly whipped out a fresh one. Then she buried her red nose in it and sobbed. "I just…I can't stand it, you know?"

Megan patted her slim back and stroked her soft blond hair and made soothing noises of support and understanding.

Finally, Carly pulled herself together enough to announce, "It's final today. Our divorce. Greg and I are…no longer husband and wife. It's over. Officially. Completely. Kaput."

"Carly. I'm so sorry…."

Greg Banning, Carly's ex, had moved out months ago—well, actually, Carly had kicked him out. As a gesture of fury and defiance. Because he'd asked her for a separation. She'd kicked him out and started calling herself by her maiden name.

But it had all been pure bravado. Carly wanted him back. Desperately. Getting her handsome husband to return to her was *all* Carly wanted, all she talked about.

No one in the neighborhood knew why Greg had asked for the split. There had been no big scenes, no angry confrontations—not that anyone knew about. Carly claimed they never fought.

But then, out of nowhere, he'd asked for a separation. She'd tossed him and his personal belongings out on the lawn of the great big house they owned that took up two lots in the heart of the cul de sac that was Danbury Way. Greg had left and never come back.

The neighbors assumed there must be another woman. But no one had seen such a woman, or had a clue who she might be.

Carly dabbed at her wet cheeks. "I know I shouldn't have locked myself in here. But I couldn't stand it downstairs. Everybody's being so *sweet* to me, feeling so sorry for me. And then there's Rhonda and Irene. Those two just won't leave me alone. You know how they are. Like vultures, hanging around, picking at the bones of everybody's troubles…."

Rhonda Johnson and Irene Dare were the neighborhood's most notorious gossips. They lived around the corner, next door to each other, on Maplewood Lane.

"Those two," said Megan, with a dismissive wave of her hand. "Ignore them."

"Oh, I'm trying. I truly am. But every time I turn around, one of them is standing there, looking so *sympathetic,* whispering how I should tell her everything, every little detail, and she won't breathe a word to another soul…. I mean, they shouldn't even *be* here. It's *our* block party, not theirs." Carly sniffed. "Okay." She blew out a hard breath. "That was petty of me. That was just downright *small.*"

"It's all right…."

"No. Danbury Way parties are always the best

ones. Everybody in Rosewood knows that. I can't blame Rhonda and Irene for coming. I just wish they'd leave me alone."

"I totally understand."

Carly's soft lip quivered and her china-blue eyes filled again. "Oh, Megan. If only he would call me. If he would just *talk* to me, you know?"

Megan dared to suggest, "Maybe it's too late for that. Maybe what you need to do is to start finding a way to get over—"

"I just don't understand." Carly cut in, shaking her head, oblivious to what Megan had been trying to tell her. "I'll never understand. I've been the perfect wife to him. He's the center of my world. I know I could make everything right between us, if he'd only…" A sob escaped her. "…only…" Her eyes brimmed. "…give me a chance…" And she dissolved into tears again, crumpling toward Megan in her abject misery.

Megan dropped the box of tissues and gathered her close. Carly sobbed all the harder. Megan stroked her soft blond hair and whispered that everything was going to be all right. Eventually, Carly wound down to a sniffle and a sob or two.

Just when Megan was about to take her by the shoulders and tell her it was time to dry her eyes and rejoin the party, someone knocked on the door. Carly gasped and snapped up straight. Megan called, "Try the master bath," and whoever it was went away.

But Carly did get the message. She heaved another big, sad sigh and pressed her palms to her flushed, damp cheeks. "Oh, I'm such a mess. I have simply got to pull myself together. We can't stay in here forever. It's just plain rude. And I was not brought up to be rude."

Megan smiled. She really did like Carly, who was always the soul of courtesy and Southern gentility— even today, when her perfect marriage to the perfect man was over in the most final kind of way. "Come on. Splash a little cold water on your face, smooth that gorgeous hair and let's get out there where you can show Irene and Rhonda that they don't get to you in the least."

Carly took another tissue and dabbed her eyes. "Megan. Thank you."

"Hey. Anytime." She started to rise.

Carly caught her arm. "Wait."

As she sank back to the edge of the tub, Megan sent a little prayer winging heavenward that Carly wouldn't turn on the waterworks all over again. "What?"

Carly straightened her delicate shoulders and hitched up her chin. "I'm calling Greg."

Megan blinked. "Well, if you really think you—"

"No, silly." Carly actually smiled. "Not for me. For *you*."

Megan wasn't following. "I don't…why?"

"Your company. What's it called? Design…?"

"Design Solutions."

"Yeah. That's right. You're a…?"

"I'm a graphic designer." And Design Solutions

was all hers. Megan had a staff of six—okay, five and an intern. Her office was a short train ride away, in Poughkeepsie, close to home with low overhead.

Carly was nodding. "You do, um, brochures, business cards, flyers, things like that, right?"

"Right." Megan did a lot more than flyers and brochures. But whenever she tried to explain about the real scope of effective design, about branding and positioning and how a top designer could boost a corporation's bottom line, her neighbors tended to get glassy-eyed. As a result, except for Angela, no one in the area really understood what Megan's work was all about.

It was kind of funny, really. The neighborhood wives were always trying to help her out. They had her designing invitations to their kids' parties, making flyers for their charity yard sales, creating letterhead stationery for their own personal use, that type of thing. Then they'd slip her a fifty in payment and tell her how "talented" she was.

Megan knew they meant well, that they were only trying to be supportive. But they saw her in a certain way; she was the nice "full-figured" girl who rented the apartment over her sister's garage.

They didn't understand that she *had* owned a house three years ago, a house she'd sold so she could put all her money into starting up her business—*and* help her single-mom sister out with the kids.

Megan's business venture had taken off. In a big way. She hardly had time anymore for a good night's sleep, let alone for small jobs at nominal fees.

Carly muttered darkly, "Yeah. It's the least Greg can do…."

Megan realized she hadn't been paying attention. "Excuse me?"

"He can give you an interview. He can maybe hire you to do…the things you do."

"Hire me?"

"For Banning's. You know. You can be their, um, graphic designer."

Megan was all-ears by then. "You're serious."

"Oh, yes I am." Carly sniffed and forced a brave smile.

"Wow…." Banning's was a small but nationally known family-run chain of upscale department stores. *This* was a real opportunity. Landing the Banning's account would be a coup. And Megan would love a chance to freshen up their slightly stuffy image.

Carly reached out and patted her hand. "I'm grateful. I truly am. For those times, like now, when you've been there, to listen to me and comfort me when things have been so rough for me. You are a very sweet person, Megan, and I want to do *something* to pay you back for your kindness to me."

Megan returned Carly's smile. "What can I say, except 'wow' all over again?"

"I'm glad to help you out…." Carly's long lashes fluttered down and her forced smile softened. Megan knew she was thinking that asking Greg for this favor would be a good excuse to get in touch with him.

Megan also knew that Carly—and Greg Banning—would see this as strictly a mercy interview. Banning's would, of course, already have a major design firm overseeing all their graphics and company-image print work. Greg would agree, for his ex-wife's sake, to hear Megan's pitch, all the while knowing he would end up politely turning her down.

What Greg Banning didn't know was that Megan was Good—capital *G* intended. She was taking Carly's offer and she was going to knock Greg Banning's socks off.

In a purely professional sense, of course.

Megan realized that she, like Carly, was looking down. Because there *was,* after all, the little matter of…

The crush.

The embarrassing truth was that, back when Megan used to see Greg now and then around the neighborhood, before he moved out on Carly and into an apartment in the city, Megan had had a slight—very slight and totally secret—crush on him.

A crush that was completely over and didn't matter in the least. Puh-leese. In his own rich-guy-next-door way, Greg Banning was a complete hunk. He was so far out of Megan's league there was no need to even *think* about that silly crush. It wasn't as if he'd ever paid the least bit of attention to Angela Schumacher's dumpy sister. Even ordinary guys never did….

Now, wait just a minute! The voice of the new, successful Megan Schumacher piped up in her mind.

True, before Design Solutions, Megan had often wished that she wasn't so shy, that she was prettier and thinner, that some nice guy might notice her.

Now, though?

Not so much. Lately, she was feeling much more confident on the man front. When Megan was in entrepreneur mode, dressed in the bright colored, snug power suits that she favored, men often looked twice. Some flirted, some even put moves on her.

Not that it made a whole lot of difference in her day-to-day life.

Between her booming, yet still fledgling, business and her commitment to help her sister with the kids, Megan was on the go 24-7. Even if she met someone who interested her more than her career, where would she find the time to be with the guy?

Uh-uh. Right now, romance was just not on her agenda.

And the slight—and so *over*—crush on Greg Banning would be no problem. This was business. Period. And it would be a major feather in Megan's professional cap to bring in her team and create a whole new image for Banning's, Inc.

"So, then," said Carly. Megan turned her head to find the other woman watching her. "You do want me to do it—to give him a call for you?"

"Yes. Thank you so much. I'd love a shot at a contract with Banning's."

"Great. I'll call him. You can consider it done."

Chapter Two

On Monday, July 3, with Independence Day looming, most of the businesses in Manhattan's financial district had gone ahead and called it a four-day weekend. At the offices of Banning's, Inc., a lone receptionist held down the fort at the desk by the elevators. And Greg Banning, president and CEO, sat alone in his bright corner office, tying up a few loose ends without the usual workday bustle and noise to distract him.

He could have been elsewhere. He'd had invitations. Since becoming a bachelor all over again, Greg had discovered that there were a lot of good-looking, smart women who were more than willing to go out with him. Hey. He was a Banning. That meant money and influence and that made him a catch.

But Greg wanted something not just any sophisticated, beautiful woman could give him. He wanted…

Okay. He wasn't sure exactly what he wanted. But he knew what he *didn't* want: a woman who was after him for his name and his bank account.

So instead of a lawn party upstate or a four-day weekend in the Hamptons, Greg had opted for the temporary quiet of the city and the pile of work always waiting on his desk. He'd given his personal assistant the day off, had a clear calendar and didn't expect to be disturbed.

But then, at eleven, his phone buzzed. Surprised, he checked the display: the security desk down in the lobby. Was the building on fire?

Frowning, he punched the talk button. "Greg Banning."

"Mr. Banning, Megan Schumacher is here to see you."

Megan Schumacher? Who the hell was…?

Then he remembered. Damn. Carly had called him two weeks ago and asked him to interview Angela Schumacher's sister. He'd agreed, and had gently gotten rid of Carly. And then promptly forgotten all about it. Which was why the appointment—for today, at eleven—had never made it to his calendar.

Greg scoured his brain. Megan Schumacher…

The woman lived over the Angela's garage, didn't she? And she was in…?

Graphic design. Yeah. According to Carly, she

owned a small company, the name of which escaped him. Carly had asked him to consider using Megan's little company for Banning's design work.

Greg just hadn't been able to tell her no. He felt bad for Carly. He honestly did. He felt bad and he felt guilty—which was why he'd made sure she got a nice, fat divorce settlement and why he couldn't refuse her when she asked him to interview her friend from the neighborhood.

Greg straightened his tie and shook his head. What a damn waste of time—both his and the poor Schumacher girl's. Banning's already had the services of a top-notch graphic design firm at their disposal. It was a firm Banning's had been using for over twenty years, a firm that invariably delivered a quality product on time and within budget.

So there was zero chance he would hire Megan Schumacher. And that meant all he could do right now was smile and make nice and let the poor thing down gently.

"Thanks. Send her up." He punched the line to the receptionist's desk. "Jennifer, Megan Schumacher is coming up to see me. Show her the way to my office."

"Of course, Mr. Banning."

Greg hung up and went back to the flow chart he'd been studying. A few minutes later, Jennifer spoke from beyond his wide-open door.

"Mr. Banning, Ms. Schumacher is here...."

Greg clicked the program shut and glanced up. The sexiest woman he'd ever seen was standing in the doorway. Greg blinked. "Uh. Thanks, Jennifer. That's all." The receptionist left them.

And the incredible woman in the doorway greeted him with a glowing, dimpled smile. "Greg. How've you been?"

Simple question. But somehow, he'd temporarily forgotten how to speak.

Superlatives scrolled through his stunned brain: amazing. Outstanding. Exceptional...

Not pretty, really. *Better* than pretty.

She was full-figured in a hot-pink jacket and skirt, an outfit that hugged her generous curves. She wore one of those camisole things under the jacket; he spotted a tempting hint of black lace that matched her sleek black high-heeled shoes. Her blond hair fell in soft waves to her shoulders.

Could this possibly be Angela Schumacher's nondescript little sister?

Evidently.

He couldn't believe it. He *remembered* Megan Schumacher—or rather, he *didn't* remember her. To be brutally honest about it, all he could recall of her was a general, fuzzy impression of someone shy and plain and slightly overweight.

But *this* woman...

She literally sparkled with energy and life and...well, there was that word again: *sex.*

He really needed to stop thinking about sex.

Greg was a conservative man. He kept his flirtations away from the office, never mixed business with pleasure, had never gotten near another woman while he was married to Carly.

But right then, in the first five seconds after this new, astonishing Megan Schumacher entered his office, all of his fine principles flew right out the window. He *wanted* her. Damned if he didn't. He wanted her bad.

And he'd been sitting there gaping at her like a teenage kid with his first big-time crush. He jumped to his feet. "Megan. It's great to see you."

She dimpled at him again. "Admit it. You barely remembered me. And I can see it in your eyes. You promised Carly you'd give me this meeting—and then you instantly forgot all about it."

Ouch. She'd nailed him.

No point in denying it. "Okay, you got me," he confessed as he stepped out from behind his big glass desk and crossed to meet her. She carried a large, soft briefcase and a hefty portfolio. He took the portfolio from her with his left hand and extended his right. "But now you're here and so am I. And I can't wait to hear all about what Design Solutions can do for Banning's."

She sent him a conspiratorial glance, one that hinted she thought he was laying it on a little thick. But all she said was, "Good. Because Design Solutions has a lot to offer you." Her perfume tempted him—flowers, plus something slightly tart. And more than the flowers and the tartness, she smelled of…

Peaches. Damned if she didn't smell like a sweet,

ripe peach. Her hand was soft and smooth and cool. He liked the feel of it cradled in his. Liked it a lot.

He had to remind himself to let go. "Your company is relatively new, isn't it?"

She nodded firmly. "Design Solutions is three years old and growing by leaps and bounds. I have two graphic artists on staff, a Web expert, an office manager, a clerk-receptionist and an intern who helps out wherever we need him. I'm looking at bringing in another artist and possibly even a second designer at the first of the year." She gestured with one of those soft hands. "Just put the portfolio down anywhere." With the tips of her fingers, she brushed the back of one of the two chairs that faced his desk. He wished those fingers were brushing *him*. "Sit here, beside me. I'll boot up my laptop and we can get started…"

Sitting beside her.

Excellent idea. He took the chair she'd indicated and propped her portfolio up on the floor between them, then he sat back and watched as she took a laptop the size of Cleveland from her fat briefcase and opened the thing on the outer edge of his desk.

"I'll show you some of the work we've done." She sent him another of those captivating smiles as the big screen glowed to life. "Then I want to give you a basic idea of the many ways Design Solutions can bolster and expand on the Banning's brand. Finally, we'll take a look at a few things in the portfolio. It's always good, I think, to get a sense of textures and colors, to see firsthand how the print work is going to translate. We can do so much online and with computer programs now, but sometimes digital images simply aren't the same as holding the finished product in your hands…."

"Excellent," he said as she started bringing up examples of work her company had done. Each one was different from the last, and each was terrific—clear and well-organized, with colors that popped and graphics that jumped right off the screen.

As she began explaining how she would work her own particular magic on Banning's image, Greg realized he was interested—and not only in the lush, peach-scented Ms. Schumacher herself.

Her ideas for Banning's were fresh and exciting. And Greg *had* been thinking lately that the company needed an upgrade on the image front. Their trademark black-and-red graphics had once seemed sophisticated and dramatic.

Now, though, gazing at the images Megan had prepared for him, the plain black-and-red seemed a little bit tired, didn't it? A little bit *old.*

"We don't want to go with different colors," Megan suggested. "We don't want to lose your brand recognition. We just want to…update your look a little. Instead of midnight black, we'll make it just a tiny bit silvery. So the black has a certain…luster. No?"

He was nodding. She continued, "And we'll go from that slightly blue red to an even brighter, more aggressive true red…."

"I like it."

She glanced at him. That dimpled smiled

bloomed and her green eyes danced. "I kind of figured you would."

She spoke of launching a print campaign to make sure all of Banning's customers were aware of the fresh styles they carried now. They needed, she said, to showcase the new clothing lines they'd recently introduced, the ones that targeted a younger, trendier consumer. She took apart Bannings.com, said the pages were too slow to load, and navigation could be simpler. Her Web guy, she promised, was a genius. He could get with Banning's Web people and help them streamline the site while they worked on the various image-brand issues.

Greg listened and nodded, asked a few questions and liked the answers he got, all the while planning how he was going to get to know her better.

It might not be easy. She was direct and cheerful and friendly. But she wasn't coming on to him. Not in the least.

Still, she had to feel it, didn't she? The heat of attraction? She was only behaving appropriately, hiding her personal interest in him, keeping it strictly business, right?

Or was interest on her part no more than wishful thinking on his?

He just plain couldn't believe that he'd once lived on the same street with her and never even noticed her. She was not the kind of woman a normal, red-blooded man easily forgot.

She wrapped up her presentation, and by then he

was totally sold. He would have Design Solutions revamp the image of Banning's department stores.

But there were more steps to take before he could tell her she had it locked up. Greg's father, Gregory, Sr., chairman of the board of Banning's, Inc., would have to be convinced, as would a couple of the vice presidents. Greg had no doubt that Megan and her team would cinch it with the rest of them, but he wasn't telling her that. No way. If he told her, she might just smile that stunning, dimpled smile, say "Thank you very much," and leave.

"I want to hear more," he said, as she zipped up her portfolio. "It's almost one. Are you hungry?"

For the first time since she'd strolled so confidently through his office door, she looked doubtful. A slight frown formed between her smooth brows. She cleared her throat. "Well, I…" The words trailed off.

He jumped right in before she could find a way to say no. "Let me take you to lunch. You like Italian? I know a great little Italian place up on Lexington at 33rd. The food is terrific and the service is, too."

For a moment—barely a split second—he thought she looked…what? Shocked? Wary? Slightly frantic?

But before he could decide what the look might mean, it vanished. She flashed him another of those incredible smiles of hers. "Why not?" she said. "Lunch it is."

Megan was having the time of her life.

She had so aced her presentation. Soon, there

would be more meetings with more executives. She and her team would need to get right on a formal Flash presentation—one that would blow them all away.

Oh, yeah. She would get the Banning's account, she just knew it. And now here she was, sitting next to Greg on gorgeous, glove-soft black leather in a company limo.

Greg had insisted on the limo, so she could stash her big portfolio and heavy briefcase in the trunk and forget about them while they were in the restaurant. Megan enjoyed a limo ride as much as the next girl. What was not to like?

She leaned on the padded armrest and gazed out the smoked-glass window at semideserted Manhattan streets. "I love New York on days like this."

"You mean when everyone else is gone for the holiday?"

"Exactly." She turned to Greg, met those velvety brown eyes of his and told herself that the thrill that shimmered through her every time she looked at him didn't mean a thing. "It's so…peaceful. For a change."

"Your offices are in Poughkeepsie, you said?"

She nodded. "Close to home and economical. You live here in the city now, don't you?"

"Yeah. I've got a loft apartment right on Broadway, two and a half blocks up from the office."

"Convenient."

"That's what I tell myself…." He had a great voice. Deep. Smooth as melted chocolate. But did he sound kind of…wistful?

She thought of Carly, wondered as she'd wondered more than once in the past months just what had gone wrong there—two beautiful people with everything going for them. Two *nice* people. Really, their breakup made no sense.

Megan dared to suggest, "You sound...I don't know. As if you're not happy living in the city."

His warm gaze cooled just a little. "I'm happy. Perfectly. And here we are...." The limo rolled to a stop in front of the restaurant and the driver got out and opened the door for them.

"Thank you, Jerry." Greg pressed some bills into the driver's palm. "We'll be awhile. I'll call for you when we're ready to go."

"Good enough, Mr. Banning." Jerry tipped his chauffeur's cap and got back behind the wheel.

After the heat of the summer day, the restaurant was cool and dim and inviting. The hostess called Greg by name and took them to a corner table. Even with half of Manhattan out of town, the place was almost full. "Must be popular," Megan said to Greg once the hostess had left them.

"It is. Deservedly so." The wine steward appeared. He and Greg conferred briefly. The steward nodded and left, reappearing a moment later with bottle of chenin blanc. There was pouring and tasting. Finally, the wine guy left. Greg held up his glass. "To Design Solutions. Much success."

Oh, well. One glass wouldn't hurt. And she was pretty much finished working for the day, anyway. She touched her glass to his. "To success." She sipped. The wine was excellent. "Umm. Wonderful. Too wonderful…."

"Is that bad?"

She couldn't help laughing. "Not in the least."

He leaned a little closer across the snowy white tablecloth. "You are amazing. You know that?"

A curl of alarm tightened inside her. She ordered it gone. He wasn't putting a move on her. No way. It was just a compliment. No big deal. "People from the neighborhood are always surprised when I happen to run into them during working hours."

"On Danbury Way you always seemed so…"

She laughed again. "I believe the word you're looking for is shy? Or maybe bland? Or just plain dumpy…"

He pretended to look injured. "Did I say that?"

"You didn't have to—and I confess, okay? In the neighborhood I do like to, er, play it low key."

He sipped from his wine. "Why?"

"Habit, I guess. And, oh, I don't know. Everyone at home sees me a certain way. And I don't disillusion them."

"But if it's not the real you…"

It seemed so natural to lean toward him, to brush the back of his hand with light fingers, to enjoy the lazy, pleasured feel of that brief touch. "But it is the real me."

He frowned, though his eyes had a teasing light in them. "Then who is it I'm sitting across from right now?"

She shrugged. "This is me, too."

"Ah," he said, but he still looked doubtful.

She explained further. "They're *both* me. I guess this is more the *new* me—and at home, I'm pretty much the *old* me. If that makes any sense."

"I'll take the new you."

Before she could come up with a suitably light-hearted reply, the waiter appeared.

After they ordered, Greg asked how she'd come to live over her sister's garage. She explained about wanting to put everything she had into starting up her company. "That was three years ago," she said. "And Angela and her ex, Jerome, were calling it quits. My moving into the apartment at her house worked out for everyone. Angela and the kids can use the extra money I pay in rent, and I get a nice, reasonably priced place to live. I can zip back from Poughkeep-sie at four most days and stay with the kids after school until Ange gets home from work. Then, if I have anything that won't wait, I hop the train and head back to the office to put in a few hours in the evening."

And why was she telling him all this? As if it mattered in the least to Greg Banning how she and Angela juggled child care and the necessity of bringing home a paycheck.

He remarked in a tone that said he really was interested, "Sounds like a tight schedule."

"It is. For both Angela and me. But we manage…."

"You're smiling. I think you love your sister a lot."

"Yeah. I do. She's my best friend."

"Any other sisters? Brothers?"

"Nope. Just the two of us—in fact, I was adopted into the Schumacher family when I was eleven and Angela was thirteen...." It had been a very tough time, those first years after her parents died. Megan had been bounced from one foster home to the next.

"Your birth parents?"

Was this getting just a little too personal? Probably. But then again, none of it was any deep, dark secret. "I was seven when they died. We went on a family vacation in the Bahamas—my parents, my brother and me. Mom and Dad rented a boat and took us out on the ocean. A sudden storm blew in. The boat capsized. I survived by catching a piece of driftwood and holding on until help finally came. My parents and my little brother...not so lucky. They said it was a miracle that I lived through it, that they even found me...."

Funny. After all these years, it still got to her, to remember the ones she'd lost so long ago. If she closed her eyes, she could almost hear her mother's warm laughter, see her father's loving smile. She'd adored her bratty brother, Ethan, even though he could be so annoying.

Not much remained to her of the day she had lost them. She recalled that the sun had been shining when they set out. The sky had darkened. And after that, she had only a series of vague, awful impressions of clinging to that bit of driftwood in an endless, choppy sea, calling for her mother, her father and Ethan until her throat was too raw to make a sound....

Greg's big, warm hand settled over hers on the white tablecloth. She looked down at it—tanned, dusted with golden hair, strong and capable looking. It felt really good, to have him touching her.

Much, much *too* good...

She eased her hand away, picked up her wineglass and knocked back a giant-size gulp.

Greg's dark eyes held sympathy and understanding. "What a horrible thing to happen—to anyone. But especially to a little girl."

She beamed him a determined smile. "Well. I got through it. And eventually, the Schumachers adopted me. Angela and I hit it off from the first. And then, three years later, our parents divorced. It was pretty bad, especially for Angela, who'd had just about the perfect childhood up till then."

And come on. Megan had said way more than enough about herself and her childhood. "What about you?" She was reasonably sure he had no siblings, but she asked anyway. "Brothers? Sisters?"

He was shaking his head. "I'm an only. I grew up in a brownstone on the Upper East Side. Big rooms in that brownstone. And high ceilings. Kind of empty, really. And very, very quiet."

She sipped more wine. "Your parents still live there?"

"Yes, they do."

"You wanted brothers, didn't you? You wouldn't even have minded a sister or two."

"Yeah. I wanted a houseful of brothers and sisters. Didn't happen, though. Truthfully, for my mother, one child was more than enough."

Vanessa. That was his mother's name. Megan knew this because Carly had told her. Carly said Vanessa was tall and slim and very sophisticated. And difficult to please. "Greg's mother never did like me much," Carly claimed. "Not that she's happy about Greg wanting a divorce. Vanessa doesn't believe in divorce, so she's on my side for once. But it's not for my sake or anything. It's just the principle of the thing, you know? She's always made it painfully clear that she would have preferred it Greg had married some rich Yankee woman from Vassar or Bryn Mawr, instead of me...."

The waiter appeared with a pair of calamari salads. He set the plates before them, poured them each more wine and then was gone.

Megan picked up her salad fork and popped a bite into her mouth. She wasn't a big squid fan as a rule, but the salad was wonderful. She chewed and swallowed, thinking about Carly, feeling just a little bit guilty about the way things were going here. This was a business lunch, and nothing more. But somehow, it was a business lunch that felt way too much like a date.

They both concentrated on the fabulous food for a moment or two, in a shared silence that was surprisingly companionable. Megan sipped from her water glass and decided a change of subject—away from the personal and more toward the professional—was in order.

She suggested, "We haven't set a date and time for our next meeting."

He sent her a look, one that heated her midsection and curled her toes in her best pair of shoes. "We aren't finished with this one yet."

She toasted him with her wineglass. "I like to plan ahead." And she took another sip, though she knew she shouldn't. She was on her second glass and the world was looking a little bit soft around the edges. Plus she was smiling way too much. That always happened when she drank more than one glass of anything with alcohol in it. She became a smiling fool.

Greg took a sip, too. "Okay. Tell me what you've got in mind."

Firmly, she set down her glass. "A formal presentation. With my entire team there—and anyone from Banning's who you think should be in on the final decision."

"That sounds like the next step to me."

"I'd love it if you and your people would come up to Poughkeepsie for the presentation."

"You want it on your turf."

"I do." She was grinning again. Much too widely. But somehow, she couldn't—or wouldn't—make herself stop. "Would that work for you?"

"When?"

"A week from today. Say, 10:00 a.m.?"

"That's quick."

"We're not only good, we're efficient."

"I like efficiency." His eyes said there were other

things he liked, things that had nothing to do with updating Banning's brand.

She remembered her objective. "So…?"

He nodded. "Next Monday at ten in your offices. That should work. I'll need to check with the others, confirm that they can make it."

"I'll have my assistant call your assistant, just to firm things up."

Those dark eyes gleamed. "You mean to make certain the date and time get on my calendar."

She shrugged. Eloquently. "Well. There's that, too."

"I won't forget. Not this time. How could I? After all, it's an appointment with you."

An appointment with you….

His tone *was* personal. And so was that gleam in his eyes. Megan knew she should say something, should make it clear right then and there that, for Carly's sake, she could never allow anything personal to go on between them. At the very least, she should sit up straight, stop leaning toward him across the table, stop smiling into those beautiful eyes of his.

But she said nothing. And she went on smiling, went on leaning eagerly toward him, went on wishing with every fiber of her being that he wasn't Carly Alderson's ex.

Chapter Three

Greg wanted to stay in that restaurant forever, to sit across from Megan and stare into those clear green eyes, to listen to that slightly husky voice of hers and try to make her laugh. She had the best damn laugh, free and full-throated.

But after she refused dessert and finished her coffee, well, he could see that she thought it was time to go. He called Jerry and paid the bill and they went out into the glaring brightness of the afternoon.

"Take the limo," Greg said.

She looked adorably bewildered, those round, soft cheeks slightly flushed, and confusion in her eyes.

"But there's no point. I can catch the train right here at—"

"You're not taking the train. Jerry will take you home to Rosewood—or on up to Poughkeepsie, if that's where you're headed from here."

"Oh, I couldn't...."

He caught her hand. Heat sizzled up his arm. "Yes, you could."

She swallowed, pressed those sweet lips together—and then broke into a smile. "Well, okay then. I'll take the limo gladly. And thank you." Since he still held her hand firmly in his, she shook it, pumping her arm up and down with great enthusiasm.

He finally got the message and reluctantly let her go. "You're welcome." He opened the limo door for her. She ducked inside. He shut the door. She rolled down the window and smiled up at him.

He passed her his card, the one with all his numbers on it—office, cell and home. "Next Monday."

She took the card. "Ten o'clock." Those lips of hers seemed to beg for a kiss.

"Gotcha." He tore his gaze from her mouth to keep himself from doing something completely unacceptable. "Till then..."

She nodded and rolled up the window. He tapped on the passenger window. Jerry rolled it down. Greg passed the chauffeur another big tip. "Take Megan upstate. She'll tell you where."

"Will do, Mr. Banning."

Greg stepped back from the car. The limo rolled away from the curb. He stood staring after it until it turned the corner.

As the hot afternoon faded into a muggy evening, Greg began to wonder what the hell had gotten into him. Damned if he hadn't gone completely gaga over Angela Schumacher's sister. He'd come *that* close to dragging Megan out of that limousine and into his arms. *That* close to kissing her—a hard, long, wet kiss—right there on the street.

Maybe it was the wine….

But he knew it wasn't. He'd been long-gone over the woman from the moment he'd glanced up from his computer and found her standing in the doorway to his office. There'd been no wine then. He'd been stone-cold sober.

Unbelievable. Unacceptable. And impossible.

He was never going to go out with Megan Schumacher. She was from the neighborhood, for pity's sake. She lived three houses up from Carly….

No way. Couldn't happen. If he and Megan started seeing each other, there would be talk. And Carly would be hurt even more than he'd already hurt her.

Greg would never go back to Carly. It was over between them and had been for a long time. He did, however, feel a certain…tenderness toward her. A certain responsibility. She *was* a good woman, just not the woman for him. Somehow, sweet Carly Alderson had turned out to be the perfect wife. Greg didn't want perfect. He'd *never* wanted perfect. He'd grown up with perfect and it was a cold, sterile way to live.

He knew that Carly had yet to accept that it was over. But in time, she would. Until then, though, he owed it to her to stay away, to keep himself the hell out of her life—which meant *not* dating someone she considered her friend. Whatever had happened to him at the sight of sexy Megan Schumacher, it couldn't be allowed to happen again.

Greg stood in the darkness of his apartment and stared out at the Manhattan night and considered calling Megan to tell her he'd changed his mind about using Design Solutions.

But no. That would not only be a bad business decision for Banning's, it wouldn't be right. Her work was top-notch. Her ideas were brilliant. She'd never been anything but strictly professional during the meeting and the lunch that followed. *He* was the one who'd come within an inch of stepping over the line.

Megan deserved this opportunity. And he had zero doubt that once his father and the others saw what she could do, she would get the contract. They'd be lucky to have her.

Uh-uh. It wasn't Megan Schumacher's fault that Greg Banning had gone crazy over her. It was Greg's problem and he would handle it.

From now on, when it came to Megan, Greg was keeping his mind on business and business alone.

* * *

In Rosewood late that night, Megan lay in her bed and stared at the silvery half-moon out the window and thought the same things that Greg was thinking seventy-five miles away.

How could this have happened? She'd truly believed that the silly crush she'd once had on Carly's husband was over. And yet, since she'd left Greg on the street outside the restaurant, she couldn't stop thinking of him. His name played over and over in an endless loop inside her head: Greg, Greg, Greg…

Which was dumb, dumb, dumb. She didn't need a boyfriend. She didn't have *time* for a boyfriend. Her life was jam-packed and then some. She hardly had time to get her legs waxed. There wasn't a minute left over for romance—especially not for a romance with Carly Alderson's ex.

This was bad. Megan was way too attracted. Much more attracted than she'd been back when Greg and Carly were married. Then, it had only been a kind of now-and-then dreamy fantasy of what it might be like *if*…

And now? Well, to reiterate: Greg, Greg, Greg…

But it didn't matter. This crazy feeling she had for him was going nowhere. When she saw him next Monday, she'd make sure it was business and only business.

Period. End of story.

* * *

"Pancakes, pancakes. I love pancakes...." Michael sang the words and then poked a great big wad of pancake, dripping syrup, into his mouth.

"Eeww," remarked Olivia. "You've got syrup on your chin and it's rude to sing at the table."

"We're not at the table," Michael corrected with the pure and literal logic of a five-year-old, the words mushy with that mouthful of pancake. He swallowed. Hard. "We're at the breakfast counter." Angela's roomy kitchen had an L shaped eating area along one section of the main counter.

"It's the same," insisted Olivia. "The breakfast counter is the same as the table when it comes to singing—so you just quit it."

"Pancakes, pancakes," Michael sang some more.

"Mo-om. He's sing-ing." Olivia turned on her stool to stick her chin out at her mother, who stood by the electric griddle down at the end of the counter, flipping another batch of blueberry pancakes.

"Eat your breakfast, honey," said her mother. "And Michael, stop singing and finish eating."

"Humph." Michael forked up another huge bite and shoved it in his mouth. Olivia flounced around to face front again and delicately picked up her own fork. Anthony ate in silence, staring at his plate.

The doorbell rang. Anthony's head jerked up. "It's Dad!" he crowed, brown eyes suddenly alight. "He's early." Jerome was due at ten to take the kids to the Catskills for the day.

"Dad!" echoed Michael around a half-chewed lump of pancake.

"Gross," muttered Olivia.

And then, in unison, all three kids announced, "I'll get it."

"Stay put." Megan slid her napkin beside her half-empty plate. "All of you."

Olivia groaned. Michael shrugged. Anthony let out a big, fat sigh. But they all remained on their stools.

In the foyer, Megan pulled open the door and found Carly on the front porch looking absolutely gorgeous. Her blond hair fell in soft, perfect waves around her beautiful face, which glowed with just a touch of blusher and a dab of lip gloss. She was dressed in the spirit of the day, in trim, royal-blue capris and a curve-hugging white shirt. On her perfectly manicured feet she wore a pair of strappy red sandals. She carried a layer cake on a crystal cake stand.

The cake was almost as stunning as Carly, a good eight inches high and slathered in ivory-colored swirls of buttercream frosting, with an accurate depiction of an American flag drawn in colored icing across the top.

"Wow." Megan was so impressed with the cake she almost forgot to feel guilty about going love-wacko over Greg. "*That* is beautiful."

Carly blushed and smiled her prettiest smile. "I baked it for you and Angela and the kids. It's a red velvet cake. And if I do say so myself, it is delish. Where I come from, we would always have red velvet cake on Independence Day."

Megan ushered her inside and shut the door. "Come on back to the kitchen. We're having blueberry pancakes. There's plenty. Join us."

"Oh. No. Really. I can't. All I have to do is *look* at a pancake and I put on five pounds."

Megan, who always did a lot more than look at her pancakes, only shrugged and offered, "Coffee, then?"

"I'd love a cup. Yes."

They went on to the kitchen, where Angela spotted the cake and said, "Oh, Carly, you shouldn't have " Even the kids got all wide-eyed over it— well, except for Anthony, who only got wide eyed lately when his mostly absent dad was at the door.

Carly took a stool, accepted a cup of black coffee and talked to each of the children in turn, asking them how they were doing and what their plans were for the day. Michael peppered her with a volley of questions. Olivia, whose rock collection was her pride and joy, solemnly explained that her grandpa had sent her a real quartz crystal, a big one, all the way from Arkansas. Even Anthony opened up to her a little. He said his dad was coming and they were going to the Catskills Game Park and maybe there would be fireworks after dark.

Carly was good with kids. Megan couldn't help wondering why she and Greg had never had any.

Not that she would ask. Oh, no. Not going there. No way...

The kids finished their breakfast, cleared their

places and ran upstairs to get ready to go. Angela served herself the final stack of flapjacks and sat at the counter while Megan got the coffeepot and gave all three of them refills.

Carly, sitting between Angela and Megan, sipped and said how good the coffee was, and asked Angela how her job managing that dentist's office was going.

Angela said it was great. "And I get holidays. All the good ones. What more can I ask for?"

Regular support checks from Jerome would be nice, Megan thought. But of course, her sister would never say that.

Megan knew what was coming. After a moment, it did.

Carly turned to her and sweetly scolded, "You didn't call me yesterday to tell me how it went. Did Greg hire you?"

Keeping her expression totally noncommittal, Megan shrugged. "Not yet. That was just the preliminary meeting. There will be a more formal presentation at my office next week, with my whole team involved. There'll also be Gregory, Sr., and a few vice presidents, I think."

Carly let out a cry of delight. "Look at you. So calm and collected. I mean, you just said 'Not yet.' Why, he *is* going to hire you, isn't he?"

"Surprised?" Megan couldn't help teasing.

"Well, I…I just…"

Megan smiled. "Hey. It's okay. I can't tell you how much I appreciate your setting up that interview." *Too bad I went and fell for the guy you're still in love with.…*

"Oh, well." Carly's thick lashes swooped down. "I was happy to do it."

"I'm very grateful. The chance to land the Banning's account, that's a big deal for me."

Carly sipped more coffee. "So tell me. How *is* Greg?" Her cheeks were pinker than ever and those Delft-blue eyes glittered with a frantic kind of hope.

"Well, of course, it *was* a business meeting," Megan hedged, and felt like a low-down, backstabbing creep. "But he seemed well. You know, healthy. All that…"

On Carly's other side, Angela looked up sharply from her plate of pancakes. She'd always had a sixth sense about what was going on with Megan. Megan lifted an eyebrow and Angela lifted one right back.

Carly was oblivious to the sisterly signals. "Did he seem too thin? I worry, you know? That he's not eating right…"

"Uh. No. He looked okay. Fine. Really."

"What did he say about me?"

Good googly moogly. Megan honestly couldn't recall his mentioning Carly's name once. "Nothing. Really." Carly's face fell. And Megan heard herself adding, "He sends his regards, of course." *Liar, liar, pants on fire…*

"His *regards*…" Carly mulled that over for a moment, her full lower lip quivering just a little.

"Yes," Megan said, so cheerfully it set her own teeth on edge.

Carly pasted on a smile. "Well. That's something. I guess…." She popped off the stool as if she'd been ejected from it. "And you know what?" She tugged on the hem of her crisp white shirt. "I really do have to get going. I only meant to stay for just a moment. My, how the time does fly." She was halfway across the kitchen already.

"Bye, Carly," said Angela, with another sharp look at Megan. "Thanks again for the amazing cake. We will totally enjoy it."

"My pleasure." Carly's voice was tight. She ducked out through the dining room.

Megan trailed her to the door, where Carly paused, swallowed back the tears that were shining in her eyes, and asked, "Your next meeting with Greg and his dad and the executives, when is that?"

"Monday."

"Well, you'd better call me afterward this time. Promise?"

"I will."

She reached up to smooth her perfect hair. "I want to hear all about it, now. I mean it."

Since the meeting next Monday was going to be business and nothing but, Megan told herself, she had zero to worry about. "You bet."

Carly's forced smile widened. "Good luck."

Megan thanked her again, and at last she left.

Back in the kitchen, big sister was waiting. "Okay." Angela pushed her plate to the side and picked up her coffee cup. "What the heck is going on?"

Megan picked up her own cup and leaned against the counter. "Absolutely nothing."

Angela gave a tiny snort. "Liar."

Megan scowled at her sister. Leave it to Angela to cut right to the chase. "Really. It's nothing." Because I'm not letting it become *something*.

Angela wasn't buying. "Something happened. With Greg Banning…" Megan winced—and her sister had one of those lightbulb moments. "Oh. My. Gosh." She sent a glance over her shoulder, as if checking to see if Rhonda Johnson or Irene Dare or some other neighborhood busybody might be lurking there. And then she whispered, "You and Greg…?"

Megan plunked her cup down and crossed her arms over her midsection. "No. That's not so. I'm telling you, nothing happened."

Angela patted the stool that Carly had vacated. "Sit. Now."

With a put-upon sigh, Megan took the stool. "What?"

"Exactly *what* happened while nothing was happening?"

"I gave the presentation. I was terrific."

"Of course you were."

"He said he wanted to hear more…."

"Yeah, and?"

"He asked me to lunch—and don't get that look. Nothing was said, you know? He didn't…make any moves or ask me out or anything."

"Well, he asked you to *lunch*."

"Angela. Come on. Sometimes Dr. Zefflinger takes you to lunch. Does that mean he's putting a move on you?"

"Dr. Zefflinger is happily married, not to mention almost sixty."

Megan blew out a breath. "Not my point."

"Oh, really?"

"Ange. Business colleagues go to lunch all the time. It's perfectly acceptable—in fact, a nice lunch is a good way to get to know the people you're working with. It doesn't have to be a man-woman thing."

Angela looked at her long and hard. Then she nodded. "Right. It doesn't have to be. But this is."

Megan lowered her head and groaned. "Why is this happening?"

Angela waited until she raised her eyes again. "You really like him. I mean, you really, *really* like him."

"Why are we talking about this?"

"Because you need to talk about it."

"No. I don't."

"Yes, you do—and you said he didn't ask you out?"

"He didn't. I don't believe he will. I believe he's going to think it over, the way *I've* been thinking it over, and decide that it's a terrible idea for him and me to ever…get together."

Angela frowned. "Wait."

"What?"

"Well, what did he *do* to let you know he was interested? I mean, if taking you to lunch doesn't count. If he didn't say anything or do anything, if he didn't come on to you…"

"Oh, please. You know how it is, the little things

a guy does, the…electricity in the air, when there's attraction."

Angela made a face. "I'm a single mom with almost no free time. I wouldn't know a date if it fell on me. I work for a pediatric dentist who, as I just pointed out, is sixty and very married to his wife of forty years. Let's just say I've forgotten, okay? Refresh my memory."

"Arrgh."

"Come on. Fill me in."

"He…um, well, in the restaurant, he put his hand over mine when I told him about how my birth parents died— and then he didn't take it away. I had to kind of slide my own hand out from under it. And earlier…that first moment when I walked in his office. Oh, Ange." Megan put her hand against her fast beating heart. "You should have seen his face. Shocked. Amazed. Awestruck. Thrilled. Excited. All of the above. And I felt the same way. But I covered it. Pretty well, I think. I was the soul of professionalism."

"Oh, I know you were."

"…Until those last few moments outside the restaurant, before he sent me home in the limo."

"He gave you his limo—to come all the way to Rosewood from Manhattan?"

"Farther. To Poughkeepsie. I went on up to the office. I tried to give the driver a big tip, but he only shook his head and said that Mr. Banning had already taken care of it."

Angela's eyes were saucer-wide. "Well, okay. I'm convinced. I mean, his *limo*..."

"Exactly."

"So what happened? On the sidewalk, before the limo?"

"Oh, I don't know." Megan's cheeks were flaming. She pressed her hands to them to cool them a little. "It was just...I just knew he was going to kiss me. And oh, did I ever want him to do that. He grabbed my hand again. And, same as in the restaurant, he didn't let go. I considered just, you know, kind of throwing myself against him. But I controlled myself. Thank God for that."

"And you'll see him again next Monday?"

"Yeah."

"And if he asks you out then...?"

"He won't."

"Go with me here. What if he does?"

"Well, I'll have to say no, of course."

"Why?"

"Oh, come on. You know why. Because it wouldn't be fair to Carly. Because it would be so cruel."

"Megan. The fact is, Carly and Greg are divorced. Not separated. Not *getting* a divorce. They are no longer married and they aren't together in any way. They're through."

"But Carly hopes—"

"It's not your fault what Carly hopes. Greg hasn't been on Danbury Way since she threw him out of Tara." The rest of the houses on the street were colonials. But Carly's huge house, with its tall pillars and wide front veranda, looked like something out of *Gone with the Wind*. The neighbors referred to it either as Tara or, more commonly, the McMansion. "He's not coming back. Carly needs to accept that her marriage is finished, and get going on the rest of her life. She's a beautiful woman, inside and outside. And it's a shame that she's throwing her life away waiting for a man who's gone for good. You're not doing her any favors by turning Greg down for her sake."

"But…you know how people talk. She'd be mortified. And even worse than all the gossip, she'd think I went behind her back and went after him when she was so sweet and got me the interview in the first place."

"So don't go behind her back. If he asks you out and you decide to go for it, the classy way to handle the situation would be to speak frankly to Carly about it."

Megan's stomach felt as if a big, hard fist was squeezing it. "To *tell* her that I'm dating Greg…."

"That's right," said Angela.

Megan cringed and Angela saw it. She spoke more gently. "It wouldn't be such a terrible thing for you, either, you know? If for once in your life you went after what you wanted instead of always going along with what everyone else wants."

"I go after what I want."

"In your work, yes. But on Danbury Way…?" Angela answered her own question with a shake of her golden head. "Look. Just think about it, okay?"

"I can't, Ange. I won't. I'm not getting anything going with Greg Banning, so there's no reason for me to ever talk to Carly about it."

Chapter Four

From the moment Greg walked into the bright, high-ceilinged offices of Design Solutions in the heart of downtown Poughkeepsie, he knew all his firm resolutions meant zip. There was no way he could keep things strictly business with Megan Schumacher.

That day she wore purple. Stunning, bright, gorgeous purple with a hint of white lace under her short, form-fitting jacket. He took one look at her flushed, adorable face, saw the little dimple in the curve of her cheek and realized it was hopeless.

He was sorry about Carly, sorry he didn't love her anymore. Sorry that in the neighborhood there would no doubt be talk about him and Megan. Sorry that

Carly would probably end up suffering more than she'd already suffered.

Yeah. He was sorry.

But Megan was…

Words failed him.

He only knew that he had to take his best shot at getting closer to her. When the deal was made and he could get rid of his father and the other Banning's executives, he was taking her to lunch—and after lunch, he was doing everything in his power to convince her to stay at his side until dinner. And after dinner, to get her to see that they should go home to his place and she should stay the night. In the morning, there should be breakfast. And lunch tomorrow. And an intimate dinner tomorrow night.

Was that crazy?

He hoped so. Greg Banning had been waiting all his life to go crazy over the right woman. And now that he'd finally found her, he wasn't letting the chance for a little glorious, happy, wild, wonderful insanity slip through his fingers. Not without one hell of a fight.

He introduced her and her team to his father and to the three dark-suited Banning's vice presidents. She spent a few minutes detailing the qualifications of each of her people, explaining the jobs they all did and how each would contribute to the update of the Banning's brand.

They dropped the shades and dimmed the lights for the Flash presentation, which was every bit as convincing as he'd expected it would be. Once the show was over, the secretary brought in refreshments. Two hours of brainstorming and Q&A followed.

Those were informative, important hours. Greg gave his full attention to the task at hand. At the same time, he longed for it all to be over. He couldn't wait to get busy convincing Megan that the two of them had a lot more than business to transact.

It all went off beautifully. Design Solutions won the contract. Next, it would go to legal. Megan, her Web guy and her senior graphic artist would come down into the city on Friday to firm up all the details.

Of course, after the meeting, his father insisted on taking everyone to lunch. But Megan was one step ahead of Gregory Banning, Sr. She had reservations at a really good seafood place right on the Hudson a few miles from her office.

It was after two when his father and the three other executives finally climbed into the stretch limousine and headed back to Manhattan. Greg sent them off without him, explaining that he'd take the train down later, as he had a few more points to go over with Megan.

He didn't mention that the "points" in question had nothing at all to do with Design Solutions or the big job Megan and her team had just been hired to accomplish. Why should he? They—especially his father—didn't need to know.

Not yet, anyway.

Megan had called a couple of cabs to get her

people back to the office. He took her aside as the others climbed in.

"Stay. Please. I need to talk to you."

She looked flushed, suddenly. And bewildered. A whole other woman from the smart, savvy entrepreneur who'd just sold Banning's, Inc. on a complete image makeover. "But I didn't plan to—"

He cut in—fast—before she could find a way to say no. "You really *need* to go back inside that terrific restaurant with me."

"Um. I do?"

"You need another cup of coffee. Or maybe a glass of wine."

"Oh, no. No wine." She looked really scared.

And that made him smile. "Coffee it is, then."

"But—"

"Stay right there. Don't even move."

She actually did what he'd told her to do, stood there on the sidewalk as he paid the two cabbies and sent her employees on their way. Then he took her arm—hours and hours he'd been waiting for the chance to do that, to take her arm, to clasp her hand....

He took her arm and he turned her and led her back inside, where the hostess gave them a little table tucked away in a corner. It was quiet in the restaurant by then. Nice, in that easy time after lunch ended and before the dinner rush began. The waitress brought them cups and cream and sugar and served them from a silver pot.

When she left them alone, Megan slanted him a look from under her lashes. "All right," she said, both breathless and grim. "What?"

He didn't know how to begin. Yet surprisingly, when he spoke, he found he sounded sure. And confident. "I think you know."

And she did know. She sighed and looked down into her full cup of coffee as if regretting that she would never taste it. Finally, after it seemed to him he had waited forever, she met his eyes again. "Oh, Greg, I don't think we can. I'm sorry. But Carly's my friend and I can't stand to hurt her."

"Listen," he began. When she started to speak, he put up a hand. "Just let me say this. Okay?"

She swallowed. "All right."

"I told you that I was an only child." He waited for her to nod. When, reluctantly, she did, he forged on. "What I didn't say is that my parents are..." Damn. What was the word for them? "Cold, maybe. Distant. To everyone—including each other. I honestly don't think I've ever seen them touch, except in passing. Never a kiss or a hug, no public displays of affection of any kind. Banning is an important name in New York. And my mother was born a Wright—one of the Philadelphia Wrights. Their wedding was the biggest social event of 1972. Over the years, I've come to think of what they have together as more of a merger than a marriage."

Megan nudged her untouched coffee to the side and rested her forearms on the table. "Your father did seem a little...cool."

That made Greg chuckle. "Cool? He *almost* smiled once during lunch. For my father, that's big.

Huge, even. Trust me. Today, he was as warm and friendly as he gets."

She glanced down, briefly, and then looked up again to search his face. "So it was tough for you, is that what you're saying—as a kid, I mean?"

"Tough?" He shrugged. "After hearing how it was for you—losing your family at seven, going into foster care—I know I've got no room to complain. I had everything."

She was shaking her head. Her smile was tender, full of true understanding. "Everything but someone to hug you—and love you."

He took a sip of coffee and replaced the cup in the china saucer with care. "I hated our house. So big, so quiet, so expensive and perfect and…empty. I was mostly raised by nurses and nannies. Once a day, in the evening before bed, my mother would stop by the nursery for a visit. She was always dressed for dinner when she came. I wasn't allowed to touch her, except for a quick peck on her perfectly made-up cheek before she left. I hated that. I hated my life.

"But I was…well-behaved. I was the heir to Banning's, Inc. and I did what was expected of me. I got good grades at prep school, went off to the University of North Carolina at Chapel Hill for college, where my dad had gone and *his* dad before him. They have one of the top business programs in the country. I was a senior, planning to stay another two years and go on through the MBA program, when I met Carly."

Megan winced. "Carly," she said too softly. And then she looked away. "Greg. Honestly, there's no need to go into all this."

He spoke quietly, leaning close so no one else would hear. "You think I want to talk about Carly, to…dredge all this up again? Believe me, I don't. But I think this is the stuff that has to be said."

Megan did meet his eyes then. And she sighed. "All right. Go on—you met Carly in college…."

"She was on full scholarship, a freshman in library science. It was at a fraternity party, the first time I saw her. She'd come with a roommate. She was so beautiful and so…I don't know. Unspoiled, I guess. We started dating. She was different than any girl I'd known. Sweeter, more…open. Or so I thought."

Megan frowned—and jumped to the defense of her friend. "Carly *is* sweet. She's one of the nicest people I know."

"I agree," he said, and meant it. After all, it was only the truth. "She's very sweet—a nice woman. But open? Uh-uh. Carly has secrets. There are… walls she puts up that no one gets through. Or at least, that *I* never could get through. And take my word for it, I tried. I really believed we would be happy, you know? That we would have a houseful of wonderful, messy, loud, rambunctious kids…."

He let his voice trail off. The point was to help Megan see what it had been like with Carly, make her understand *without* making excuses. Mindful of that objective, he tried again. "Once I'd finished school, we moved to Rosewood." He smiled to himself, remembering. "I love Rosewood. To me, it's the ideal place to live. I was sure I wanted to settle down there the first time I visited, when Carly and I were house-hunting and went to have a look around."

Megan almost smiled. But she was keeping it serious. He watched her quell that smile before it burst wide open. She said, "You *love* Rosewood?"

"Yeah. You think that's strange?"

"Well, I mean, I agree it's a great town. Mostly upscale. Good-quality housing. But it's hardly one-of-a-kind. There are a lot of towns upstate that are very much like it."

"I don't know. Rosewood just says 'home' to me. It's the best kind of place to live, clean and attractive. The streets are safe. The schools are top-notch. It's a town any man would choose as *the* place to raise his family."

"And that was what you wanted. A family. A big one…"

"Yeah."

"And Carly didn't want kids?"

"She said she did. But she kept putting it off— until it was too late. Whenever I mentioned getting started on our family, she would say she wasn't ready. First, she said the house we bought wasn't big enough for a family. We bought the house next door, tore our house down and built Carly's dream house on both lots. Once the house was built, I brought up the idea of kids again. She said she wanted the house to be perfect first...." There. He'd said it. The *p* word. He repeated it. "Perfect. That was always the main push with her. Carly wanted—*needed*—for things to be perfect."

"...And you'd already had more than enough perfection to last you a lifetime."

He sat back in his chair. "See? You get it. You get it, exactly. Carly wanted it all to be perfect—and I wanted anything but. It was sad, really. The timing was never right for Carly and me. At the end, when it was too late for me, *then* she started making those 'let's have a baby' noises. And by then, I could only say no, that our marriage was in trouble and we needed to deal with that first—at which point she'd clam right up on me, paste on a bright smile and change the subject. I felt...sympathy for her. Even then. I honestly did. She wanted so badly to please, you know?"

Megan was nodding, her eyes so soft. "Yeah. I know."

"She was always dieting like crazy, to get into her size two designer clothes. She knocked herself out trying to get my mother to like and respect her. I told her that would never happen, that Vanessa Wright Banning didn't *like* anybody and only respects people she considers above her on the social scale. But Carly kept trying. She just wouldn't quit. She took cooking lessons and became a gourmet chef. I'd come home every night to a four-course meal straight out of *Bon Apétit* magazine—a meal Carly herself would hardly touch. And then there was her family...."

Megan looked thoughtful. "You know, she's never mentioned her family to me."

"To me, either."

"Wait a minute. I don't think I'm following."

"I'm saying that to this day, I know pretty much zip about the Aldersons. Carly's family was always off-limits between us. When I'd ask about them, she'd either change the subject or find some other way to evade the issue. I wanted to get to know them a little, to see the town where she grew up. There was always some reason why we couldn't go there. I met her mother, Antoinette, once. Can you believe that? Once. At our engagement party. Some family emergency came up and Antoinette couldn't make it to the wedding. I never had a damn clue *what* the emergency was, even. Carly just said there was one. No details, no explanations."

Megan was quiet for a moment. What was she thinking? He couldn't tell. Finally, she said, "I'm sorry, Greg."

He didn't feel the least encouraged by her tone. "What does that mean?"

"It means I wish it had worked out for you and Carly. I truly do." Megan's voice was low. And much too careful.

And suddenly, he felt anger rising. "You know what? Being sorry isn't going to make everything okay again. I hate that it turned out this way, because I always believed that when I said 'I do,' it would mean forever. But Carly and I just weren't right for each other. We were after completely different things.

Our marriage is over. There won't be any trying again."

"I understand."

His heart sank. The regret in her eyes told him clearly what was coming. He went ahead and prompted her. "So…?"

"Greg. I get it. I honestly do. You're not going back to her. You're divorced and you're free to date anyone you want to date."

He laid it right out there. "I want to date *you* "

"Well, that won't happen. Carly thinks of me as a friend. And that means I can't go out with you."

He swore quietly. "You know that's just crap, don't you? You think you're protecting Carly? You're not. And you're not helping her, either."

Megan said nothing. And Greg got the message: it didn't matter what he said. She wasn't going out with him. Period.

Finally, he muttered, "I guess we should go." He reached for his cell phone to call them a cab.

Outside, as they waited for the taxi, Megan was careful not to stand too close to him.

In the restaurant, it had been so hard for her not to lean across the table, not to get as close to him as she possibly could. She really did love to…just be with him. To watch him as he talked—his crooked, wry smile, those warm brown eyes, the way he would tip his head to the side when he was thinking. More than once, as he told her about his lonely child-hood and his failed marriage, she'd had to remind herself not to reach across the table and lay her hand over his.

Greg turned to her as the cab slid to the curb in front of them. His mouth, usually so quick to smile, was now a bleak line. "One more thing…"

She didn't know if she could take any more—not and keep remembering to tell him no. "Oh, Greg…"

"There's something I want you to see, okay? In Rosewood. Let me take you there. Please."

She reminded herself that she needed to repeat all the things she'd already said—that she couldn't. She wouldn't. It was impossible; it wasn't going to work.

But his brown eyes were shining and the summer sun struck gold lights in his thick brown hair. And, well, he'd asked her so gently. So very sincerely.

If she was never going to go out with him, well, what could it hurt to do this one last thing he'd asked of her?

Not to mention she was curious. What could he have to show her in Rosewood? She dared a smile. "All right. I'd love to see it…whatever it is."

His face seemed to light up from within. "Well, okay, then. Let's get after it."

During the ride to Rosewood, they hardly spoke. Megan, who didn't feel all that chatty herself, looked out her side window at the suburban sprawl and thought about the things Greg had said in the restaurant.

They pretty much amounted to what Angela had told her last week. Greg and Carly were divorced.

The marriage was over for Greg; he was never returning to the McMansion on Danbury Way. Megan's saying no to him wouldn't help Carly to get him back—or to get on with her life, for that matter.

In fact, if Carly finally had to accept that there was another woman in Greg's life, it might actually end up making it easier for her to move on. From that angle, Megan would be doing her a favor by going out with Greg.

Yeah, right. Megan seriously doubted that Carly would see it that way.

When they reached Rosewood, Megan asked the cabbie to drop them at the train station so she could pick up her car. Greg said they were going to Sycamore Street, which was only five blocks from Danbury Way. She sent him a suspicious glance, but he wouldn't say more, so she started up the car and off they went.

When she turned onto Sycamore, he pointed at a fine-looking two-story house, redbrick with white shutters, on the west side of the street—a Federal-style colonial, like most of the houses in the neighborhood.

"Pull into the driveway," he said.

The driveway curved around to a side-entry garage. The door began rolling up as they approached it.

Megan let out a surprised laugh. He showed her the opener he had in his hand. She teased, "Do the owners know you've stolen their garage-door opener?"

"Very funny. Drive on in."

She tapped the gas and the car nosed into the empty space. Greg pressed the button on the remote; the wide door rolled down behind them. She turned off the engine. "Who lives here?"

"No one, at the moment."

"This house is yours?"

"Yes, it is."

"It's beautiful—from the outside, at least."

"I think so."

"Complete with white picket fence and a matched pair of sycamore trees on the front lawn."

He looked so pleased with himself. "Don't forget the white shutters."

"I noticed those. And that cute brick walk that leads up to the front steps…"

"It all just says 'home' to me."

"Well, yeah—in a totally upstate New York suburban kind of way."

"See, that's exactly what I was going for."

"When you bought it, you mean?"

"Yeah."

"And when was that?"

"A week after Carly threw me out."

Megan realized she was leaning across the console toward him—as he leaned toward her. An inch or two more and they'd be kissing, for heaven's sake.

She bolted up straight and asked just a little too forcefully, "So. Are we going in?"

He watched her for a moment, his face unreadable, as her heart beat too fast and her breath tangled in her throat. And then, with an easy shrug, he slid the remote in a pocket—and came out with a key. "You bet we are."

She waited as he unlocked the door that led inside, and then followed him into a combination laundry room and pantry. A window over the laundry sink looked out on a big backyard.

Greg took a moment to deal with the alarm, then began randomly opening cabinets. "Nice hardware, don't you think? And lots of storage space."

She played along with him, keeping it teasing and light. "Absolutely. I can't think of a better laundry room, anywhere."

"I knew you'd say that." He was probably a little bit closer than he should have been. She got a hint of his aftershave—and found it way too tempting.

She moved back a step and gestured at the twin blank spaces beneath a row of cabinets. "Wouldn't hurt to get a washer and dryer, though. Hard to do the laundry without them."

"Good thinking."

"And a personal touch or two, that would be nice. Maybe a few houseplants, a little greenery in the window…"

"Great idea." He closed the distance she had just opened. "I'd already thought of the washer and dryer. But the houseplants hadn't even occurred to me."

"And laundry supplies. Those are a must."

"Laundry supplies," he repeated in a musing tone. "Detergent, bleach…" She realized she was looking at his mouth. He had a really fine mouth—a slightly fuller lower lip and a kind of pensive curve at the corners...

"I'll start a list," he said in a low voice.

"Yes. Good. A list..." And once again they were practically touching. Why, if she stretched up tall and moved her head forward a couple of inches, she could press her lips to his.

But of course, she wasn't going to do that. She didn't even know why such a thought had dared to creep into her mind. Twice. First out in the car and now here, in the laundry room.

Uh-uh. No way.

"Megan?" His voice was soft. Would his lips be soft, too, if she were to kiss him?

Bad question. Irresponsible question. She had to stop thinking about kissing him.

He said her name again, even more softly than before.

"Um. Yeah?"

He was almost smiling—as if he knew exactly what she was thinking. "Would you like to see the kitchen?" He gestured toward the open door.

"Terrific. The kitchen." She turned and stepped through the doorway into a roomy breakfast nook with a picture window that looked out, like the one in the laundry room, on the backyard. "Very nice."

"Lots of light," he said from behind her, and the sound of his voice seemed to vibrate all through her, it was so warm. And much too exciting.

She stared at the granite-topped peninsula that

marked off the kitchen area. "A Viking cooktop," she said on an exhaled breath. "Impressive."

"Sub-Zero refrigerator," he murmured, still behind her—*closer* behind her, as a matter of fact.

She felt the naughty smile as it tugged on the corner of her mouth. "Next you'll be telling me that's a Bosch dishwasher."

"Two of them."

"No…"

"Yeah. See? On the opposite side of the sink?"

"Wow."

"It's the latest thing. For busy families and time-crunched executives. You can live your whole life without ever putting the dishes away. You use them straight from one dishwasher, loading them into the other until it's full. Then you switch." He stood right behind her now. "I'm all for efficiency." His whisper was as intimate as a caress.

"Uh, yeah. Me, too." It took all the willpower she possessed not to lean back against him with a surrendering sigh, not to give in to the potent desire to feel those strong arms of his closing around her. "I love the light fixtures, too," she said, breathlessly.

"That pleases me no end—that you like them."

"I do." *I do?* Was she out of her mind? Telling Greg Banning *I do?* This had to stop. She needed to…turn around, for crying out loud. Turn around and face him.

Somehow, she mustered the gumption to do just that. She turned and found herself looking straight at his power tie and his strong, tanned neck. She cleared her throat.

"What?" he said. Though she was looking at his tie and not his face, she knew he was smiling. She could hear that smile in his voice.

She tipped her head up and met his eyes. Gorgeous eyes. Standing so close, she could see a rim of ebony around the brown irises and little rays of gold coming off the dark pupils. "Time to...move on."

He nodded. Slowly. "You got it." And again he gestured—this time through the kitchen area to the arch that led to the dining room. She turned and pointed herself in the direction he'd indicated.

In the dining room, she admired the hardwood floor and the simple craftsman-style stained glass chandelier that hung over the place where the table should have been.

Before he could move too close and get her thinking about kissing him again, she kept going, into the great room, with its big brick fireplace, cherry mantel and twin tall windows looking out on the front yard.

"Beautiful," she said, and, "Very nice," as they moved through the central hallway.

He pointed at a shut door. "Half bath," he stated. "A must."

He sent her a look that managed to be both humorous and sexy. Big trouble, oh, yes. She kept her mouth shut and answered his look with a shrug. He led her on to the master suite.

She didn't linger there. Uh-uh. Even without a bed to get her thinking of all the intimacies she was never going to share with him, the master bedroom was still a dangerous place for the two of them to be.

She hurried on into the master bath. "Two sinks. A necessity."

"Yeah. I thought so, too."

There was also a huge shower and a sunken tub more than big enough for two, complete with spa jets.

Oh, my, yes. Too dangerous for words. With a smile and a nod she slipped past him, back out into the empty bedroom. She admired the walk-in closet and the roomy dressing area. And then, at last, he ushered her out of there.

The front hall was spacious and welcoming. Afternoon light, spilling in through the sidelights that flanked the front door, made the wood floor gleam.

She followed him upstairs, her hand trailing on the smooth cherry banister. There were two more bedrooms up there, each with a big walk-in closet. The bedrooms shared a central bath.

"That's it," he told her, as they stood in the upper hall, ready to go down.

"It's lovely. Honestly."

"Thank you."

"If you don't mind my asking…"

"Anything. Go for it."

"Well, why, exactly, did you buy it?"

"I told you. I like Rosewood. I keep thinking that someday I might move back to town."

"At least you've got all your window treatments," she said. "I like them. They're simple. Elegant. The plantation shutters—and the Roman shades and wood blinds. However…"

"I'm listening."

"Before you move in, better buy some furniture. And dishes. Pots and pans. Towels. Sheets. Paper goods. Food. Those laundry supplies we talked about a few minutes ago. All that."

He grinned. "You think so, huh?"

"Even two Bosch dishwashers aren't a lot of good if you don't have dishes to put in them."

"Yeah. I know. I need to get started on all that. But the truth is I just never had the heart for it."

"For buying furniture and stuff, you mean?"

"For being in Rosewood where so much went wrong for me." Once again, he was standing close. She should move back. But she didn't. He added, "I have to tell you, though…"

"Yeah?" She was sounding much too breathless again.

"There's nowhere else on earth I'd rather be at this moment, than here. In Rosewood. With you…" He moved then, a step closer still.

Too close…

Too wonderfully, deliciously close. His warm breath touched her check and he lifted a hand to brush a stray lock of hair back out of her eyes—oh, that was heaven. Just the touch of his fingers at her temple, on her cheek, guiding those strands of hair back behind her ear. She didn't *mean* to raise her mouth to him—well, not exactly. And she didn't mean to sigh in yearning. But she did.

And when she did, he lowered his mouth to hers.

Chapter Five

Megan sighed some more and swayed closer to him. He gathered her into his arms.

Now, this. *This* was heaven. Pure heaven, right here in Rosewood, New York. Standing in the upper hallway of Greg's empty house, wrapped in his arms, with his mouth—softer even than she'd dared to imagine—on hers.

He deepened the kiss, touching the tip of his tongue to the seam where her lips met. She instantly opened for him, sighing some more as his tongue brushed hers. He smiled against her mouth and that made her smile, too.

She slid her hands up over the fine fabric of his jacket, intimately aware of the heat and hardness of the chest beneath. She touched his crisp white collar, ran her fingers up the side of his throat and brushed his temples, where his hair was cut business-short.

Oh, he felt so very *good*. To hold, to touch, to kiss....

And about that...about the way the man could kiss.

How did he do it? Okay, she didn't have a whole lot of experience with kissing, but still. A kiss, after all, was only a kiss....

Wasn't it?

That would be no. Not with Greg.

With Greg, it was...different. With Greg it was so much more.

The miracle, the wonder, the beauty of his kiss was in the way he held her, so tightly and tenderly, as if he cherished her above everything and everyone. As if he'd never, ever let her go. It was in the way his lips brushed hers and then settled in, deeper, harder, hotter....

He stole her breath and stopped her heart with that kiss of his, as his tongue stroked the secret places beyond her lips, and his hands roamed her back, rubbing, caressing, making all kinds of promises. Promises that didn't need words. Promises made in the heat and the knowing pressure of his touch.

She could have stood there forever, drinking his kiss, kissing him back, feeling wanted—needed, even—feeling truly beautiful for the first time in her life.

But then he lifted his lips from hers a fraction and whispered her name. "Megan…"

And she whispered back. "Greg…"

And somehow, that did it—saying his name aloud. It made it all achingly, terribly clear.

This couldn't go anywhere. She'd told him so and he had understood her.

This was impossible.

This was not going to be.

When he tried to claim her lips again, she shook her head. She flattened her hands on his broad chest and gently, firmly, pushed him away. He resisted, but only for a moment. His arms fell—and she wanted more than anything to sway toward him again.

But she didn't. She stepped back and whispered weakly, "I'm…sorry. So sorry…"

He shook his head. "Sorry doesn't help." His lips were swollen, red, from kissing her.

She knew hers were the same. And she couldn't stay here. If she did, she'd only end up kissing him some more. "We…we have to go."

"Yeah. All right. Whatever you say." He turned without another word and headed down the stairs. She stared after him, stunned at what had happened.

Now, after that kiss, the fact that there could be no more seemed so terrible. So totally wrong…

But no. It wasn't wrong. There was Carly to think about. Carly, who trusted her. Carly, who had cried on Megan's shoulder, revealing her heartbreak as she never would have done if she'd known about this…

At the bottom of the stairs, Greg looked up at Megan, his eyes hooded and his jaw set. "I need a ride back to the station."

She shook herself. "Of course." And hurried down.

In the garage, Megan trotted right over and climbed in the car while Greg reset the alarm and locked the inner door. She started up the engine and he got in. The garage door trundled up.

Carefully, because she was shaking and didn't really trust herself behind the wheel, she put the car in reverse, peered back over the seat and slowly pulled out. Greg rolled the door down with the remote.

She backed—too slowly, with painstaking care— out onto Sycamore Street, carefully turning the wheel so the car was pointed in the right direction. She was so busy concentrating on her driving that she almost didn't notice the two women in jogging shorts and sports bras walking their matching Yorkshire terriers on the other side of the street.

She gasped when she did see them. Ohmigod. Irene Dare and Rhonda Johnson, the two biggest gossips in Rosewood.

And they had seen her with Greg.

They'd stopped, stock-still, on the sidewalk, their little dogs yapping at their feet. They gaped from Megan's face—flushed with pure guilt, she just knew it—to Greg's, and back again.

Greg waved. The two lifted their arms in unison and waved back. Megan drove on down the street.

She couldn't keep herself from looking in the rearview mirror as she turned the corner. Irene and Rhonda had not moved on. They stood in the same spot, their dogs jumping and barking around their feet. They were no longer staring, though. Now they were talking, urgently—Irene's dark head bent down to Rhonda's frizzy red one.

Dear Lord. Let this be the one time they keep their big mouths shut....

Even as Megan formed the little prayer, she knew it was hopeless. Rhonda and Irene would make sure everyone in the neighborhood—including Carly— heard about how they'd seen Megan and Greg together, coming out of that empty house on Sycamore Street.

Chapter Six

Greg stared out his side window, not speaking, as Megan drove the rest of the way to the station. She didn't know which bothered her more, Greg's chilly silence or the fact that Irene and Rhonda had seen them together.

"Thanks for the ride," he said flatly when she stopped to let him out.

"No problem."

"You've got all my numbers." He'd given her his card that first day, in the city. "Call me if you change your mind."

"Greg, I—"

He put up a hand. "Are you about to tell me you've changed your mind?"

All she could do was shake her head.

"Then don't say anything." He opened his door. "Bye, Megan."

"Bye…." She didn't allow herself to watch him walk away from her. Still shaky—and absolutely miserable—she turned her car for home. She was so absorbed in thoughts of him, of what she longed to have with him, what she wasn't going to do with him, what Irene and Rhonda were going to say about seeing them, that she got all the way home before she remembered the kids.

Forgetting the kids. That had to be a first.

Thoroughly put out with herself, she started up the car again and headed for Rosewood Park, where she collected the kids, took them back to the house, changed into her comfy at-home clothes, and kid-sat until Angela arrived from work at five-forty.

It was then that Megan had to deal with her promise to Carly: a full report on how the presentation to the Banning's executives had gone. Facing poor Carly. Now there was something Megan had zero desire to do. She almost chickened out and returned to the office to get a head start on the Banning's project.

But no. She *had* promised.

Maybe a phone call….

Uh-uh. A call would be just too cowardly and small. So she grabbed the cake stand Carly had brought over on the Fourth and headed for Tara— aka the McMansion.

As Megan walked up the wide front steps between the two huge pillars, her courage deserted her. She was just about to set the cake stand by the arched front entryway, ring the bell and make a run for it, when Carly opened the door.

"Oh! There you are."

Caught, Megan thought, trying not to cringe.

"I've been waiting to hear how it went...." Carly grabbed her by the arm and hauled her into the soaring marble-tiled foyer. "Did you like the cake? Oh, I hope you did."

Megan stared into Carly's hopeful face. *Say something.* She sucked in a big breath and laid on the compliments. "It was amazing. I think it actually tasted better than it looked. Which is pretty hard to believe, considering how good it did look."

Carly took the cake stand and set it on the foyer table. "Well. I'm just glad y'all enjoyed it."

"Oh, we did. We definitely did."

"Come on in the den...." Carly turned. Megan, longing to be anywhere but there, stared after her until she turned back, smiled so sweetly and waved her on. "Come on...."

So Megan went where Carly led her, into the most comfortable room of the huge, overdone house. "Have a seat." Carly gestured toward a leather recliner. Megan obediently dropped into it. "Now, what can I get you? Coffee? I made a simple little pineapple upside-down cake this morning and I can just—"

"No. Nothing. Really."

"You're sure...?"

"Yes. Positive."

Carly perched delicately on the edge of the couch. "Now, then." Her eyes sparkled with anticipation. "How did it go?"

"It, um, well, it went beautifully."

Carly laughed and clapped her hands. "So…?"

"It's official. We got the contract."

"Oh, my! Well, isn't that terrific?"

"Yeah, I'm pretty jazzed."

"Oh, I'll bet. Tell me everything."

So Megan launched into a description of the meeting in her offices. When she mentioned Gregory, Sr., Carly sat forward. "How *is* Gregory?"

"Well, he liked what we had to show him. But I can't say he's the most outgoing guy in the world."

Carly looked serious. "Yes. It's true. He's a… difficult person to get to know." Carly's frown deepened. She seemed vaguely distressed.

"Are you…all right, Carly?"

She blinked. "Oh, yes. Fine. Go on…."

Megan did, wrapping it up as quickly and simply as possible, ending at the point when the Banning's executives got in their limousines and headed back to the city. She totally failed to mention the central fact that Greg had stayed behind.

Instead, she waited, certain that Carly was going to ask about Greg, and promising herself that she wouldn't lie, that she'd tell the whole truth and face the music right there and then.

But Carly only said, "That's great. Really great."

Guilty relief poured through Megan. "Thank you again. And, you know, I've really got to run…" She felt awful. Small. Like a liar and a coward. Probably because she was both of those things.

And Carly seemed—what? Disappointed. Yes. That was it. Disappointed that Megan had nothing to volunteer about Greg. Disappointed, but apparently unwilling this time around to actually ask about him. She offered yet again, "A piece of cake? You're sure?"

"Thanks, but no. " Megan bounced to her feet and headed for the foyer. "Just wanted to, you know, tell you how it went…."

Carly rose and followed her to the door. "I'm just thrilled it turned out so well."

"Yes. Thank you for everything. It's terrific. I'm excited." *Oh, and did I mention I'm also a big, fat liar and a snake in the grass…?*

"Glad I could help." Carly opened the door for her and Megan escaped with a quick wave and a last, lying smile.

Megan hardly slept at all that night. Guilt and shame and self-disgust will do that to a person.

She lay in bed hating herself for what she had done with Greg that afternoon, and the way she had lied, by omission, to Carly. Megan despised herself—well, when she wasn't longing for the man she was never going to have.

She relived that forbidden kiss a hundred times. And each time she did so, she promised herself she was putting Greg Banning strictly out of her mind.

Out of her mind.

Interesting word choice. Oh, yeah. Because she *was* out of her mind—out of her mind with yearning for a guy she wasn't ever going to kiss again.

About five-thirty in the morning, she finally gave up all hope for sleep. Feeling stir-crazy in her little apartment, she put on her robe and slippers and crossed the breezeway to Angela's, where she brewed a pot of coffee and sat at the kitchen island to watch the sunrise through the window that looked out on the backyard.

"What's up?" Angela stood in the doorway from the back hall, barefoot, in a knee-length sleep shirt, her soft blond hair tousled.

"Nothing." Another lie. But a tiny one, a lie that was nothing compared to Megan's lies of yesterday, when she'd sat in Carly's den and told her everything but what really mattered. "Just watching the sun come up." She gestured over her shoulder at the pot on the counter. "I made coffee...."

Angela padded over and got herself a cup. She slid onto the stool next to Megan. For a moment, the sisters stared out the window and sipped their morning coffee in companionable silence.

Megan found herself thinking of their childhood, of how she and Angela had been so close, right from the first. And then, when Megan was fourteen, right after Angela's sweet-sixteen birthday, their parents had separated—and then divorced.

Angela had been devastated. Megan, too, but not as bad as Angela. Megan had seen enough tragedy in her life by then that, to a degree, the divorce of her adoptive parents was just more of the same.

Their father, who had found another woman, vanished from their lives. Their mother became distant, wrapped up in her fury at their father's betrayal. The sisters had grown even closer through that tough time. They had each other, at least. And they'd both vowed never to lose their special bond.

Into the silence, Angela said softly, "When you want to talk about it, you know I'm here."

Megan took another sip. She continued to watch the sunrise. "Yeah. I know. Thanks, sis…."

"Anytime."

All through Tuesday and Wednesday at Design Solutions, at home in the evening and later in her apartment during the mostly sleepless nights, Megan promised herself she wouldn't even *think* about Greg.

Her promises were pointless. She did think of him. She kept waiting for the feeling that she was throwing away something wonderful to fade at least a little.

Waiting didn't help. The feeling didn't fade.

Thursday morning, she got up early again, went over to the main house and made coffee.

Angela appeared in her sleep shirt just as the coffee finished dripping. "Ready to talk about it?"

"Yeah. I guess I am."

They filled twin mugs and sat at the island. As the sun came up, Megan told Angela everything—from the private stuff Greg had shared with her in the restaurant Monday to the tour of his empty house on

Sycamore Street to the forbidden kiss. To how Rhonda and Irene had seen them, and finally to the way Megan had lied to Carly by not saying anything about any of it.

Angela waited until Megan had gotten it all out. And then she said exactly what Megan had known she would say. "Tell Carly. Tell her right away. You know you're not going to be able to live with yourself until you get things straight with her."

"Oh, God…"

"I know how you are." Angela sent her a look of fond exasperation. "At work, you're a dynamo. Nobody gets in your way when it comes to Design Solutions. But here at home…"

Megan finished for her. "I hate making waves."

"Well, in this case," Angela predicted, "there will be waves and you know it, as soon as word gets around that you and Greg Banning are seeing each other."

Megan gaped at her sister. "But I'm not seeing Greg. Didn't you hear what I just said?"

"Every word. And I don't believe for a minute that you and Greg Banning are done with each other. You're crazy about him. You light up like a fire-cracker on the Fourth of July every time you mention his name. And from what you've just told me, he's gone on you, too. Why are you trying to walk away from that? I don't get it. You're both single. You have every right to take the attraction you feel for each other and run with it."

"Well, yeah. Except for poor Carly…"

"Greg isn't Carly's anymore. It's sad she won't admit that, but still, it's a fact. Carly needs to get over Greg. And *you* need to deal with that big, fat hole in your integrity. You let Carly cry on your shoulder. That's your weakness—you know it is. In your personal life, you let people think what they want to think. People tell you all their troubles and you *let* them, you listen and you nod and make understanding noises. You hold their hands. Which is fine. Most of the time. But this time, well, it's kind of backfired on you. You held Carly's hand and you heard her long, sad story and now she trusts you. When you tell her the truth, she'll probably be very angry with you."

"And hurt. She'll be so hurt."

"She's already hurt. And I hope she gets past it. But you've got a problem of your own here and your problem is that you haven't been honest with her."

Angela had it right. And Megan knew it.

The kids came down for breakfast. Megan went back over to her place and got ready for work.

But she didn't *go* to work.

At nine, she marched over to Carly's and rang the bell.

There was no answer—at first. But then, just as she was about to ring the bell again, the door opened a crack and Carly peeked through.

"Megan!" She sounded so happy. The knife of guilt in Megan's stomach twisted deeper. Carly pulled the door wide. "Come on in...."

Grimly resigned to get the truth out once and for all, Megan stepped inside. Carly shut the door and let out a soft, nervous giggle as she patted her sleep-mussed golden hair. "Well, as you can see…" She retied the sash of her silk robe. "I'm not up and about yet. Lately, I just seem to be a hopeless slug-abed…."

"Carly, I really need to—"

"But *you*…" Carly's eyes had gone wide. "Megan. You look terrific. You should wear bold colors all the time. This bright turquoise does wonders for your skin—not to mention those pretty green eyes of yours. It's, well, Megan, this is a whole other you."

"Thanks. I was just, um, on my way to work…."

Carly took her by the shoulders. "Well, I am serious as a heart attack here. Get yourself some casual clothes in bright colors. Be as gorgeous at home as you are when you go to work."

"Um. I will. I'll do that."

"Good. Now, how about some coffee?"

"Ah, no. Thanks. I'm fine."

A line had formed between Carly's smooth brows. "Megan. You seem…are you all right?"

She blew out a hard breath. "No. Not really. I have something to tell you. Could we maybe sit down?"

In the den, Carly took the recliner. "Now, what? Tell me what's bothering you."

Megan realized there was no way she could sit down. So she stood a few feet from Carly's chair and made herself say that certain dangerous name. "It's about Greg."

Carly put a hand to her slim throat. "What? Tell me? Is he…did he say something after all, on Monday? Did he tell you he's been missing me? Did he hint that he wanted to try—?"

"No." The word came out harsh, abrupt.

Carly cringed and shrank back into her chair. "Oh. Oh, well, then…?"

"I'm sorry." Megan put up both hands in a placating gesture. "I didn't mean to be so curt."

"It's okay. But…oh, Megan. What did he *say?*"

Lord. Where to start? How to tell it? "He, um…" She decided she'd better just lay it out there. "He asked me out."

Carly made a tight, strangled sound. Her face went chalky-pale. "I…excuse me?"

"He asked me out. I, um, turned him down. But I didn't *want* to turn him down. I'm very attracted to him. I didn't expect that, to be so attracted. And I never in a million years thought that he'd be attracted to me. But, well, he is. He said so. And he, um, well, did you know that he owns a house right here in Rosewood?"

Carly was staring at her as if she'd just committed murder—or worse. "I don't… A house?"

"Yes. It's a few blocks away from here. It's empty now, but he says he really does like Rosewood and he's hoping someday to move back here."

"A house? What are you talking about? Greg doesn't need a house. He has a house. Our house. *This* house…"

Megan shut her eyes, sucked in a fortifying breath

and made herself continue. "No, Carly. He says it really is over, between the two of you. That you're divorced and that's how it's going to stay."

"No…"

"Yes—and that house I just mentioned? Well, he showed it to me."

Carly's fine nose wrinkled in an expression midway between sheer horror and disgust. "*You?* He showed *you* his house…."

"Yes. And…and he kissed me, Carly. I mean, *we* kissed. Each other. He kissed me and I kissed him back."

Carly blinked several times in rapid succession. "I don't…I can't…" She paused, collected herself, said with an awful kind of calmness, "You know what? I heard, from Irene Dare, that she and Rhonda had seen you with Greg. I didn't believe Irene. I thought she was just carrying tales, telling lies, stirring up trouble the way she and Rhonda like to do. I would never, ever have believed that Greg would…" She seemed to run out of words. She shook her head, tried to continue. "That *you* could…" The words ran out again. She swallowed. And then, with great care and a terrible, wounded dignity, she rose to her feet. She drew herself up tall and straightened her robe. "You *kissed* my husband?"

Megan put out both hands in a placating gesture. "Carly. No—I mean, yes. I did kiss him. But he's not your husband anymore and you really have to come to grips with that, I think."

Carly was shaking her head, backing away. "You…you pretended to be my friend."

"No. Carly. I *am* your friend…" Megan let her hands drop limply to her sides. "Or I was…"

"You stole my husband from me."

"No. I hardly knew him. I swear. And until the third of July, when I went up to his office for that first interview, Greg never showed an interest in me. He'd even forgotten that he'd told you he'd see me. It was just pure luck that I caught him at his desk."

"Pure luck…" Carly made the words sound like a curse.

"Carly—"

"You said you told him you wouldn't go out with him."

"Yeah. I did."

"And *then* you kissed him?"

Megan didn't even try to defend herself. "Yeah. And then I kissed him."

Carly tipped her chin high. "I don't know what to believe. All this you're telling me, it could be just lies."

"Oh, no. Please…"

"But the one thing I do know now is that you are not my friend, Megan. You are not my friend and I will never speak to you again."

"Oh, Carly. Please don't—"

"Shut up." Carly put both hands to her temples and squeezed her eyes tightly shut. "Just shut up. Shut up and get out of my house and never come back here again."

Chapter Seven

At home, there was no one.

Angela had taken the kids to day camp and gone to work. Megan knew that she should head for the office, as well.

But the awful scene with Carly had pretty much wiped her out. She went up to her apartment and sat on her bed and stared out the window that faced the backyard and wondered how she was going to manage to get through the day.

Sweet, gentle Carly had kicked her out of the McMansion and told her never to come back. Carly hated her now. That really hurt. And what hurt even more was the sneaking suspicion that maybe Megan deserved Carly's hatred.

No.

No, that wasn't true. She didn't deserve hatred. Fury, maybe. A good strong lecture for not being honest from the first.

But hatred?

Megan shook her head and let out a sad little laugh. What did it matter what she deserved? She *had* Carly's hatred. That was the bald truth.

Carly hated her. And Megan really, really needed to talk to Angela. She needed her sister's wisdom and level head. She needed Angela to tell her that yes, she had blown it royally. But now, at least, she'd told the truth and accepted the consequences.

Megan picked up the phone—and hesitated. She always tried to avoid bothering her sister at work. It was a small office and Angela was always on the go there. But hey, this was a special circumstance. She started to dial—and then thought of poor Carly.

Sitting in that big house all by herself. Who was Carly going to call at an awful time like this? For Megan, there was and always would be Angela's strong shoulder to cry on, Angela right there with her, to help her decide what to do next.

Who did Carly have? According to Greg, she was estranged from her family. And in the neighborhood, except with Megan, Greg's ex-wife always tried to put on a brave face.

How bad off was Carly right now? She'd been in an emotional tailspin for months. Could the news Megan had just dumped on her be enough to put her over the edge in the most final kind of way?

Oh, no. Impossible. Carly wouldn't…

But then again, what if she did?

Oh, God. What if she did?

Someone, Megan realized, ought to check on Carly and make sure she was okay. Someone should hold her hand, provide a listening ear and a big box of tissues. Megan would do it, if she herself didn't happen to be the problem.

Yes, she was fully aware that Angela would advise her to leave it alone. And Angela would probably be right.

But Megan just couldn't let it be. She felt too…responsible.

So she started dialing. She began with sweet Mrs. Fulton across the street. Sylvia was the wise and understanding grandmotherly type, the perfect neighbor to come calling when a woman's life and hopes and fading dreams came crashing down around her.

But Sylvia wasn't at home. Megan hung up without leaving a message. What could she say? *Hi, Sylvia. When you get this message, could you go check on Carly and make sure she's not slitting her wrists or anything?*

Uh-uh. Bad idea.

Marti Vincente, maybe? But again, no one answered. Marti and Ed were probably already at the restaurant for the day.

Next, Megan tried Jack Lever's house in hopes that Zooey, the widower's live-in nanny, might be around to run over to Carly's. No answer at the Levers', either.

Who next? Irene Dare? Rhonda Johnson? God forbid—wait. What about Rebecca Peters?

Megan looked up the number and tried it. But Rebecca didn't pick up.

Molly Jackson? Molly was a total career person. Megan really didn't expect to catch her at home, but was just worried enough to give her a try.

And what do you know? After two rings, Molly answered, "Hello?" Megan, who suddenly realized she had no idea where to begin, only gulped. And Molly demanded, "Hello? Hello? Is anyone there?"

"Uh. Hi, Molly. It's Megan. Megan Schumacher? I...well, I guess I didn't expect to get lucky and find you home...."

Molly cleared her throat and replied just a tad defensively, "I was feeling a little under the weather this morning, that's all."

Megan remembered the incident in the powder room during the block party last month. Wow. Did Molly have some awful disease or something? "Oh, I'm so sorry. I shouldn't have bothered—"

"It's perfectly all right. I'm much better now."

"But if you're sick—"

"I'm not," Molly said with finality. "As a matter of fact, I was just thinking I'd pull it together and go to work. And I will. Soon. But what can I do for you?"

"I...have a big favor to ask of you."

"Whatever I can do."

"It's about...oh, I don't even know where to start...."

Molly laughed. "I have days like that. Way too many of them lately. Days like today, as a matter of fact…and come on. Hit me with it. As I said, I'll do what I can."

"Thanks," Megan said. "Ahem. Well. You see, it started at the block party last month, when Carly offered to get Greg to give me an interview…."

"Hey, that was nice of her."

"It was. Really nice."

"How did the interview go?"

"Great. I got the contract."

"Well, hey! Congratulations."

"Thanks. I also kind of…fell for Greg."

There was a stunned silence. Then Molly asked, "Greg *Banning?*"

"That would be the one."

"Are you saying that he…fell for you, too?"

"It kind of seems that way."

"Well. No kidding…"

"No kidding."

"So what, exactly, happened?"

"Um. It was like this…." Megan told the story quickly. She hit the salient points: the instant and shocking attraction between her and Carly's ex; the way Megan had tried for days to deny that attraction. The meeting Monday in Poughkeepsie; Greg's asking her out and her telling him no; that kiss she shouldn't have shared with him. And how she'd finally gotten up the nerve to fess up to Carly just half an hour ago.

There was a huge silence on the line when she

finished talking. Finally, Molly said, "Megan, I really don't know what to say."

"Yeah, well. I understand." And she did. Much too well.

Gingerly, Molly suggested, "Maybe you should have picked someone else, you know?"

Good advice. *Excellent* advice. Just say no. Nothing simpler. And, somehow, in this case, about as easy as trying to stop an oncoming train by standing in front of it—not that that was any excuse.

Molly added, "Then again, they *are* divorced. Carly will have to learn to live with that."

"Maybe so. But as of this morning—she hasn't. Not in the least."

"She took it badly, then?"

Understatement of the year. "Very, very badly."

"I'll bet she needs a friend right now...."

"I *know* she needs a friend right now. And I was wondering—"

"I hear you. And I'm on my way over there."

"Oh, Molly. Thanks—and can you maybe *not* tell her that I called you and asked you to check on her? I've got a sinking feeling that would only make things worse."

"Gotcha."

"And will you just, you know, give me a quick call after you talk to her?" She rattled off her cell phone number. "Just so I know she's all right."

"Will do. And Megan?"

"Yeah?"

"Good luck. I have a feeling you're gonna need it."

Megan thanked Molly again and said goodbye and then sat there a little longer, staring out the window, wanting her sister beside her.

And more than her sister, Megan wanted Greg. In spite of everything, she *still* wanted Greg.

Eventually, she got up and went to work. For much of the day, her killer workload distracted her. Somewhat.

Still, somehow, in every relentless beat of her heart, it was there—her longing for Greg. She told herself she only had to hold out. Over time, the longing was bound to fade.

Molly called in the afternoon to say that Carly was all right. Her neighbor seemed reluctant to say more and Megan didn't push her.

As always, Megan picked the kids up at four and watched them until Angela got home. The sisters stole a moment in Angela's room with the door shut. Megan reported that she'd done what she had to do, that Carly knew about her and Greg.

Angela gave her a hug. "I know it was hard, Meg. But you did the right thing."

And then Michael pounded on the door crying that Anthony wouldn't play with him. Angela had to go sort out the dispute.

Megan rushed back up to Poughkeepsie, where she worked until after ten, getting ready for the trip into the city next morning. Strictly speaking, the meeting tomorrow would be to agree on terms. But the marketing execs would be there. They'd want to see progress on the Banning's campaign. Megan was determined they would have it—and then some.

When she finally got home that night, it was well after eleven and the lights were off in the main house. So much for her opportunity to have a long heart-to-heart with her sister. Megan dragged herself up to her apartment, put on her pjs and climbed into bed—where her longings and her worries took over and wouldn't let her rest.

After an hour of tossing and turning, she threw back the covers and padded into her tiny kitchen. She heated up a little milk, added some honey and sat down at the table to drink the age-old sleeping aid.

Her purse was right there on the table where she'd left it. She dragged it over in front of her, popped the clasp and slid Greg's card from the inside pocket.

Yep. There it was, his home number: 555-8346.

And wouldn't you know it? The phone was right there on the table, not two inches away from her steaming mug of restful hot milk. She picked it up.

Not that she would actually call him….

At a quarter of one in the morning? No way. Only stalkers and hopelessly lovesick fools did things like that. She set the phone back on the table. And then, just as she was giving it a small extra push, to send it out of easy reach, the darn thing rang.

The sound was shrill and strange in the quiet darkness of her kitchen. She let out a little gasp of surprise and then snatched it up and pressed the talk button. "Hello?"

"It's twelve-forty-five at night and I can't sleep.

I know the last thing I should be doing is bothering you. So call me a stalker and hang up the phone. That should do it, shame me into keeping my promise and leaving you the hell alone...."

Her throat tightened up. She gulped to loosen it and then whispered, "Oh, Greg..."

A moment of taut silence passed, then he murmured, "Did I wake you?"

She shook her head, though she knew he couldn't see her do it. "I'm sitting here at my kitchen table with a mug of hot milk and honey—and that card you gave me with your phone number on it."

"You were going to call me?" The joy and triumph in his voice made her heart feel too big to fit in her chest.

She confessed, "Well, no. I've just been promising myself that I won't."

Another silence was followed by a bleak, "I understand. Well. Goodbye, then...."

"Greg, wait!"

More silence. She started to think she'd lost him, that he'd hung up. But then he asked gruffly, "What?"

"Don't go. Please...."

He paused, chuckling deeply. "Well, all right. You've convinced me."

"I can't stop thinking about you." The damning words just sort of popped out. And she found she couldn't regret saying them.

Gently, he asked, "And is that such a bad thing?"

"No..." She traced the handle of her mug with a careful finger. "Yes. Oh, I don't know."

He chuckled again. "Well. At least that's one thing you're sure about."

She chided, "You think this is funny?"

"I didn't say that."

"Good. Because it's not—not in the least...."

"I know." His voice was soft and low. Intimate. Tender. "I've been thinking...."

She found she had to swallow again before she could speak. "About?"

"You."

She dragged in a long breath and let it out slowly as something moved through her—something warm and good. Maybe it was happiness. She heard herself whisper, "Oh."

"I don't know what it is about you, Megan. But from that first day, when you bowled me over with your ideas for Banning's..." The words trailed off.

She prompted, "What about that day?"

"Right from the first moment, I felt as if I *knew* you. As if I'd always known you. As if I'd only been waiting, forever, for you to show up, so the two of us could get on with the rest of our lives. Is that crazy?"

She couldn't help sighing. "Well, yeah. Pretty much."

He laughed again. "Then go ahead. Call me crazy. That's okay. Call me whatever you want. Just tell me you'll give it—give us—a chance."

She admitted the truth. "I can't stop thinking about you, either."

"Good." His voice was a rough whisper, one that

sent a hot shiver running under her skin. "So then. What else is there to do but go for it?"

"Greg?"

"Yeah?"

"I, um, well, I talked to Carly."

He knew what she meant. "About us." He didn't sound upset.

"Yes. This morning. I felt like such a cheat and liar, you know?"

"You weren't. You aren't."

"Well, I sure feel like one. I talked to my sister about it, about us, about how guilty I felt. Angela said I needed to get it out there, to tell Carly the truth. So I did. Finally. I told her…how you asked me out and I turned you down. How you showed me your house on Sycamore Street. And how I kissed you, even though I'd told you I wouldn't go out with you. She was…it really hurt her, Greg. She kicked me out of her house and told me never to come back."

"Megan. Damn it. I'm sorry."

"Me, too. But that's not going to make Carly feel any better. She just won't give up hoping that you'll go back to her."

"But I'm not going back to her."

"Maybe not…"

"No maybe about it."

"She didn't know about the house. I'm sorry if you didn't want her to know."

"Megan. There is nothing for you to be sorry about. Look. Do you want me to have a talk with her?"

"Do you...want to have a talk with her?"

"Not really. But I will, if you think it'll help."

Megan considered the idea—and rejected it. "No. You're divorced. You can date whoever you want, and Carly doesn't have any right to be upset about it. I think, in her heart, she knows that. On the other hand, she considered me a friend. And I betrayed our friendship."

"That's not true."

Megan felt a sad smile tug at the corners of her mouth. "Well. Thank you for defending me."

"We both know you've been trying like hell to shake me. You wouldn't have 'betrayed'—your word, not mine—Carly if I hadn't pushed you to see me."

"Whether you pushed me or not, I did go to lunch with you. Twice. I went with you to see your house. I kissed you."

"No. *I* kissed *you*."

"And I kissed you back."

"Megan."

She made a low noise in her throat. "What?"

"It's done. Carly knows. You were honest with her. Over time, she'll see that it's not fair to blame you."

"I hope so." Megan sat a little straighter in the kitchen chair. "And as for you and me..." She hesitated.

He didn't. "Dinner," he said. "Tomorrow night. I'd say we could start with lunch, but I heard a rumor that we're having it catered in the conference room. The place will be crawling with executives. No privacy at all."

"Dinner," she repeated, and realized she was on the verge of telling him yes. Then she thought of the kids. "I usually pick up my sister's kids from summer camp at four...."

"Can you get out of it, just this once?"

"I'll check with her. But Greg, I don't want to...rush anything, you know?"

"No problem. We'll take it nice and slow."

Did she believe him? Not really. Still, she agreed. "Yeah. Okay. Slow is good."

They were quiet. It was nice. Kind of easy and companionable. But exciting, too. At last, he asked, humor warming his deep voice, "You still there?"

"Yeah—and we should hang up, don't you think? Try to get some sleep...."

"I'm afraid to let you go. What if you change your mind?"

"I won't."

"Say that again."

Obediently, she vowed, "I promise. I'll have dinner with you tomorrow. If I can find a babysitter."

"All right, then. Good night, Megan."

"Good night." She heard the click on the line and he was gone.

She missed him already. How hopeless was that? She smiled to herself, a woman's dreamy smile, as she finished her lukewarm milk.

So what if Rhonda and Irene told tales about her,

if Molly Jackson disapproved of her, if Carly told everyone what a terrible person she was? Megan was taking this chance with this special, terrific guy, no matter what anyone in the neighborhood said....

Still, when she went back to bed, she found sleep impossible. Maybe because in the end, she really did care if everyone in the neighborhood hated her.

Chapter Eight

Through the morning meetings and lunch in the conference room, both Megan and Greg took special care to keep things strictly professional. More than once, though, she glanced his way and found him glancing back and...

Well, okay. For the first time in her life, Megan Schumacher was beginning to understand what all the shouting was about when it came to romance. Once she'd thought kind of wistfully that it might be nice to have a boyfriend, someone to go out with now and then, someone to take to holiday parties, someone to maybe get flowers from on Valentine's Day.

But this, with Greg—this whole *heat* thing, this warm-shivers-all-through-your-body thing, this weak-in-the-knees thing, well, she just hadn't known that romance could be like that.

After lunch, there was one more long meeting, with the lawyers included. And finally, at three in the afternoon, the deal was signed. The lawyers, including the one representing Design Solutions, took their leave.

Megan thanked her Web guy and Anita, the graphic artist she'd brought with her, and sent them both home. They'd worked their fannies off and deserved a head start on the weekend. She spent a few minutes wrapping up loose ends with the marketing people. By then, Greg was nowhere in sight.

She headed for the elevator. There were, after all, hours to kill before dinnertime. She would call him later, find out where to meet him. In the meantime, she was thinking maybe she'd go on home, after all, see how the kids were doing with the babysitter she'd hired. At home, she could freshen up a little, too, put on something more right for evening.

Her phone rang just as the elevator doors slid wide. She looked at the display as she was stepping into the car. Greg. With her heart doing flip-flops and a silly grin on her face, she answered, "What?"

"I left you alone in that conference room for ten minutes—and you disappeared."

The door slid shut. She pushed the button for the lobby. "It's hours until dinner. I thought I'd just go on home in the meantime."

"Don't. Stay."

She giggled. She couldn't help it. There was a guy in a gray suit in the car with her. He sent her a frown.

What? He didn't approve of giggling? She shrugged, turned toward the wall and spoke more softly. "Greg. I've got my briefcase and my laptop. I don't want to carry them around with me."

"It's not a problem. You can stash them at my place."

"I'm in the elevator."

"Don't go...."

The car stopped. "I'm at the lobby."

"Have a seat on that marble bench by the security station," Greg instructed as the doors slid wide again and the guy in the gray suit rushed out, in a big hurry to get wherever he was going. "I'll be right down."

"But—"

"No buts. Be there." The line went dead.

"Well, okay," she said to no one in particular as she put her phone away and edged around the three people who'd just gotten on the elevator. She found the bench and dropped down onto it, sending a smile and a nod at the guy behind the security desk.

Three minutes later, Greg came striding toward her. When he got there, he took her briefcase. "Let's go."

"Where?"

"My place."

"Honestly. I don't want to drag you away from work."

He gave her that half smile that made her heart do flip-flops. "You aren't dragging me. I'm going willingly."

"Have a great afternoon, Mr. Banning," said the guy at the security desk. Was that a knowing gleam Megan saw in his eye?

What did he think? That they were heading to Greg's for a…nooner?

Well, of course not. It was much too late for that. Noon was more than three hours ago—and it wasn't about the time of day, anyway.

They just *weren't,* that was all. Not…yet, anyway. Megan might be crazy about the handsome man at her side.

But the whole getting naked thing…

Nope. Not today.

She gave the guy behind the desk a quick, nervous smile. He tipped his hat at her as Greg led her away.

Greg paused inside the doors of his apartment building. He set down her briefcase and took her by the shoulders. "One thing…"

At that moment, with a whole afternoon and evening of just the two of them stretching gloriously ahead of her, she might have promised him anything. "Name it."

"Today. And tonight. Let's have it be just the two of us. Yes, I was married. I have an ex-wife. But for now, for today, can we just leave all that behind?"

She thought of Carly, wished things could be different, that Greg might be someone other than Carly's ex. But he wasn't. And Greg was right. They needed to let all the baggage go, share a day without shadows and guilt. "I'd say that's doable."

"Good. Then today, it's just you and me. No other woman will even be mentioned."

"Agreed." She smiled and tried not think that if there was an *other woman* here, she was it.

His apartment was gorgeous, so open and bright. Your classic downtown corner loft. Acres of hardwood floor and high, arched windows overlooking Broadway to the east and Warren Street on the north.

He offered a drink. "Ice water," she said, recalling the gleam in the security guard's eye. No liquor. Uh-uh. That could lead to…loosening up. And loosening up could take her to places she might very much enjoy going.

But she *wasn't* going—not so soon, anyway.

He got them tall glasses of water and they sat in his living area on the leather-and-chrome sectional. She kicked off her high heels.

Why not? Maybe she wasn't doing anything wild and dangerous this afternoon. But that didn't mean she couldn't get comfortable. She turned to him and tucked her legs to the side.

He offered a toast. "To Design Solutions. And Banning's. And a very profitable business arrangement."

"I'll drink to that." Ice cubes clinked as they tapped their glasses. She sipped. "Delicious."

"Straight out of the tap."

"There's just something about the water in Manhattan."

He set his water on the glass coffee table. "I take it you did find that babysitter."

She nodded and set her glass beside his. "She's sixteen and she lives around the corner. I had to pay her a bundle, but it was worth it. A whole afternoon of freedom. Every girl should have one now and then…."

He'd taken off his jacket and loosened his tie. He leaned a little closer and it only seemed natural to lean closer, too. "I love that dimple, right there—" with his thumb, he brushed the curve of her cheek, setting off a lovely series of tingles "—when you smile." He looked at her as if she were the most beautiful woman on earth.

"Greg?"

"Anything."

She couldn't help laughing. "Oh, come on. Please…"

He frowned. "What? I'm coming on too strong?"

"Well, maybe a little."

"Damn. I can't help myself."

"I admit it's very flattering…."

"But?"

"You know what? On second thought, go ahead. Adore me if you must."

He laughed then, too, a deep, rich wonderful sound. "All right, I will."

"But I'm not going to bed with you—not today, anyway." The words got out and she realized how abrupt they sounded—which had her letting out a tiny groan and clapping her hand over her mouth. "I can't believe I said that."

He grinned. "But you did." He ran a light finger

down the line of her hair, where it fell along the curve of her cheek. Her skin warmed in the wake of that skimming touch. "However you want it. It's okay with me." He leaned close enough to brush a kiss across her lips—a kiss he didn't deepen, though the truth was, she wouldn't have minded if he had.

With a hesitant finger, she traced his square, oh-so-manly jaw. "I think we should…go somewhere."

He laughed yet again and the sound sent a ripple of pleasure cascading through her. "Right now?"

"Yes."

"Because?"

"Because you make want to do things I'm not quite ready for."

They went to a movie in midtown. A heist flick with lots of action and snappy dialogue. They shared a box of popcorn and held hands and stole more than one warm, slow kiss.

After the movie, they went for a walk and ended up in the library at Fifth Avenue. On the first floor, which was called the popular library, they wandered into the rows of bestsellers. Among the *B*'s—the Browns, to be specific: Dan, Don, Sandra—Greg stopped to gather her close.

Megan whispered, "We shouldn't…." But she didn't pull away when he lowered his oh-so-tempting mouth to hers.

My, oh my. There was nothing—absolutely *nothing*—in the world so lovely as the feel of Greg's mouth on hers. He smiled against her lips, the way he'd smiled the first time he'd kissed her, in his empty house in Rosewood. He smiled and she couldn't help but smile in joyous response.

His tongue brushed hers. She sighed and let him in more fully. And by then, well, she never wanted that kiss to end. On the contrary, she reveled in it, shameless in her pleasure, though it was probably not the sort of thing they ought to be doing in the library.

She twined her arms around his neck and pressed her yearning body close against him. It was wonderful: the hardness of his chest against her soft breasts; the strength in his big, wide shoulders; that naughty, seductive slow heat pooling low in her belly.

Oh, yes. A girl could really get used to feeling like this....

She moaned—well, she couldn't help herself. She moaned and he made a low, throaty, oh-so-male sound in response. She slid her fingers up into his hair. It was so thick, the short ends blunt against her questing fingertips.

Oh, yes. It felt good. So very, very good....

In time, they did come up for air. He lifted his mouth from hers and she opened her eyes. They shared a long look—a look as deep and full of sweet, hot pleasure as the kiss had been.

Down at the end of the narrow aisle, someone gasped. They glanced toward the sound just in time to see a stocky, gray-haired lady duck toward the next row.

"Oops," mouthed Greg, grinning.

And Megan couldn't help it. She laughed out loud.

A furious, "Shh!" came from the next aisle over.

Megan clapped her hand over her mouth to keep from laughing again.

"I love your laugh," Greg whispered, and kissed her nose.

She composed herself enough to whisper back, "We'd better go."

So he took her hand and led her out of there, into the humid warmth of the summer evening. By then, overhead, between the buildings, the cloudless sky, tinged with pink from the setting sun, had begun to darken toward dusk.

Eventually, there was dinner. She had the squab and he had a thick rare filet mignon. They sat and talked for hours. She told him how she'd gotten her degree, on full scholarship, at the Long Island School of Design.

He said he loved being in the family business. He was proud of what his father, grandfather, great- and great-great-grandfathers had accomplished, creating Banning's and building it into a nationally recognized brand. He wanted to put his own stamp on the family company. Before he turned over the reins to his own son, he planned to take Banning's nationwide, to open stores in Los Angeles, Seattle, Phoenix, Denver, Dallas and the Twin Cities.

"Ambitious," she remarked.

"Yes. I am."

"And I notice you said 'son.' What if you find it's

your daughter who has the talent when it comes to the family business?"

"Then my daughter will take over after me."

Megan granted him a nod of feminine approval. "Good answer."

"Hey. If my daughter is up for it, if she's got what it takes, more power to her."

"From what you've told me about *your* father, I have a feeling he might not approve of a woman running the show—even if she is a Banning."

"If my daughter's that good, she'll know how to handle Dad—"

"Who will be very old by then, and most likely extremely crotchety," Megan interjected.

Greg leaned closer across the table, his voice low. "You seem downright determined to make it rough on my brilliant, hardworking little girl."

Megan winked at him. "You've got a point. And on second thought, maybe I've read your father all wrong. Outside of a certain…coolness, he's treated me just fine. He seems to have no problem doing business with me. And *I'm* a woman."

Greg sat back. "Yeah." Those dark eyes had gone to velvet. They made promises. Sexy ones. Dangerous ones. "You *are* a woman. No doubt about that."

She toyed with her water glass, turning it by the stem as she slanted him a look from under her lashes. Yes, she was flirting. Shamelessly. Blatantly. And you know what? It felt good. It felt absolutely terrific. "Then again," she suggested, "maybe your daughter will have her grandpa wrapped around her finger."

"I'm having trouble picturing my father wrapped around *anybody's* finger. But hey. Stranger things have happened, I guess...."

"And it *is* just possible," Megan warned, "that neither your future daughter *nor* your future son will want to go into the family business."

"Since I plan to have five of each, I think the odds are pretty good that at least one of my kids will be Banning's material."

"Ten kids." She widened her eyes in mock horror. "Didn't I tell you I always wanted a houseful?"

"Well, yeah. But..."

"What?"

"Just...whew."

He seemed amused. "Whew?"

"Yeah. Whew. As in, easy for *you* to say. I mean, given that you don't have to actually give birth to all ten of the little darlings."

He lifted one big shoulder in a half shrug. "It's open to negotiation. Ten may be a bit...optimistic."

"Oh, well, yeah. Probably. A bit."

"I realize there aren't a whole lot of women these days who want to stay at home and have baby after baby."

"After baby, after baby..."

He laughed then and she thought how the sound created a kind of glow inside her, made her feel that life was good and would only get better.

"Okay. I give in. I don't really know how many

kids I'll have. I'm hoping for at least three or four. But I could live with it however it works out. We might even adopt. There are a lot of kids out there who need moms and dads to love them."

He was so right. She'd been such a kid, once. "No argument there."

"It would all be workable. As long as I was living with the right woman."

"So then...you do intend to get married again?" She asked the question—and thought, once the words were out, that maybe she was going a little too far.

But he answered easily. "Yeah. Now, I do." *Now?* Meaning he hadn't earlier? "And this time," he said, "I plan to do it right. This time, there aren't going to be any more secrets. And no more lies." He paused and she saw the sudden shadows in his eyes.

She wanted to say something sympathetic, to encourage him to tell her more. But if she did that, they'd only be talking about Carly again....

And then the moment passed, the shadows vanished as he said with warmth and firmness, "There *will* be passion and laughter and fun and excitement. I know we'll have our rough patches. A good marriage always does. But we'll get through it. We'll have what matters."

Megan sipped the coffee the waiter had brought her. "Sounds to me like you've got it all figured out."

"I know what I want," Greg said, and the way he looked at her brought a thousand butterflies fluttering to life in her stomach. "I'm just not sure how to get what I want. Yet."

She shook her head at him. "I am not touching that. Not getting near it. Uh-uh."

He laughed again and she wondered how she'd lived her whole life without Greg's laughter to make the world seem shimmery-bright, brimming with hope and promise.

She had, quite simply, never felt like this before.

It was…something special, this crazy thing with him. Something tender and trusting. Something open and free. She felt as if he saw her so fully, saw all of her, saw the Megan she'd never quite dared to be.

Saw her. And really *liked* what he saw.

"Deep thoughts?" he asked.

She waved a hand, unwilling to try to explain just then. "Oh, yeah. A little. Sorry…."

He caught her hand. "No. Don't be sorry. Ever. Just be…you." She gave his fingers a squeeze before pulling away. And he said, "What about your niece and nephews? Tell me about them."

"Hmm. Let's see. Michael is five and he's always doing things like chewing with his mouth open and imitating anything Olivia says. Really irritates her— justifiably so. But I just want to hug him and tell him he's adorable. Somehow I restrain myself. Not so smart to praise a kid for sticking out his tongue through a mouthful of half-chewed Lucky Charms."

Greg was grinning. "I can just picture that."

"Don't. As Olivia is always saying, it's *really gross.*"

"And speaking of Olivia…?"

"She's seven. Very bright. Kind of serious. Not

big on the girly-girl frills, but definitely feminine. Her pride and joy is her rock collection."

"And the oldest? Anthony, right?"

Megan nodded. "Anthony's a little tough right now."

"Tough?"

"Silent. Kind of moody. Spends way too much time wearing headphones and playing his Game Boy. He was six when Jerome left. Old enough to have memories of what it was like to have his dad in the house."

"He misses his father."

"Yeah. And Jerome, well, he's not as dependable as he could be." She paused to sip more coffee. She was thinking that she probably should shut up about Jerome. Angela always tried not to say bad things about him. And Megan felt that she should follow her sister's lead, though personally, there were times when Megan thought the guy needed a good swift kick in the pants and a lecture about the responsibilities of fatherhood.

Greg picked up her ambivalence. "Well, all right. Enough about Jerome."

She beamed him a wide smile. "Thank you."

"Anything. To make you smile like that…"

The waiter appeared at her elbow with the coffee-pot. "No, thanks. I've had more than enough…."

Greg said they were ready for the check. It came and he paid it. And then they just sat there some more.

She told him about the tough times, going from foster home to foster home. "There was never a fit. Though I tried, oh, you cannot believe how I tried."

"To…fit in?"

"That's right. The Comptons wanted a bright child. I was a straight-A student. The Blakelys wanted a soccer player. I played forward. Not as well as someone more athletic, but I put my whole heart in it, I swear that I did. Somehow, though, it never seemed to work out. They would send me back and there would be another family. For a while. And sometimes I was in the Rosewood Children's Home. And then, at last, I went to the Schumachers."

"I'm glad. That you finally found the place you belonged."

She gave a wry grin. "Didn't I mention that the Schumachers divorced three years later?"

He swore quietly and shook his head, and she told him about how the divorce had at least brought her and Angela all the closer. "It was Ange and me against the world there for a while. But somehow, against all the odds, we managed to grow up into reasonably happy, responsible adults."

He said again how he envied her—that she had a sister. And he told her about the friends he'd made in prep school. They spoke of favorite movies and their tastes in music. She could have sat there the whole night, listening to him talk about his weakness for reality shows.

"I confess," he said, faking a mournful frown. "I love *Fear Factor.* Scary stunts and people eating things that make you gag. What more could a guy ask for?"

She admitted, "I have a secret weakness for *The Apprentice.* There's something about The Donald…"

"Maybe that sexy comb-over," Greg suggested.

"Oh, yeah. Probably it." She leaned a little closer and gestured toward the waiter, who was standing near the entrance to the kitchen wearing an expression of endless patience. "And the chairs are on the tables. We're the only customers left."

Greg frowned. "No way it's time to go."

"'Fraid so."

He left an extra tip for all the time they'd taken up the table since they'd finished the meal, and they went out into the Manhattan night.

"I should start thinking about heading home," she said regretfully once they were in a cab and on their way downtown.

He tightened the arm he'd laid across her shoulders. "My place. A nightcap. *Then,* if you feel you have to, I'll call the limo and send you home."

"Greg. Honestly. I can take the—"

He silenced her with a finger against her lips. "Shh. I'm keeping you in the city until all hours. The least I can do is send you home in comfort."

At his place, with the lights of the city gleaming beyond the tall windows, he called for the limo and then poured them each a brandy. They sat on the black leather couch, sipping, talking softly of casual things, laughing together at nothing in particular.

The limo driver checked in at twelve-thirty, and Greg said, "Stay. A little longer. The driver will wait."

But it was an hour and a half back to Rosewood. She stood. "No. Really. I do have to go."

Greg got up to go down with her, catching her hand and pulling her back before they left the apartment. He drew her close. "One more kiss…."

His lips met hers. She could have stood there forever, being kissed by Greg and kissing him back. But the driver was waiting and it was a long ride home. She pressed her hands to Greg's chest and he lifted his head.

"Gotta go."

Reluctantly, he released her.

But of course, outside, as the driver waited with the door wide, Greg pulled her into his arms one more time. She kissed him back, with enthusiasm.

And, finally, he let her go. "I'll call you," he said, folding bills into the driver's palm as she ducked into the car. She nodded and waved as the driver shut the door.

Her phone rang as the limo rolled up FDR Drive. She knew who it would be. And it was.

"I did promise I'd call."

"That's right. You did."

"Is Andy taking care of you?"

"Um, Andy?"

"The driver."

She glanced up front at the back of Andy's head. "So far, so good."

"Tomorrow," Greg said, and then corrected himself. "Wait. Make that today, since it's already Saturday. I want to see you *today*."

"You just saw me."

"It wasn't enough. Can you be ready by eleven? I'll send a car."

"You are much too extravagant. Really. I can—"

"It's nothing. Eleven. Be ready."

"For?"

"Anything. Bring shoes you can walk in."

Now, there was some great advice. Her poor feet couldn't take another day like today—not in three-inch heels, anyway. "Will do." She leaned back into the plush leather seat.

His voice was husky in her ear. "I had a great time…."

"Me, too," she answered softly, thinking that the night had a glow to it and FDR Drive had never looked so beautiful.

Megan slept like the proverbial log that night. Her dreams were sweet ones, full of sunshine and a certain man's sexy smile. She was up, showered and dressed and joining her sister in the main house at eight-fifteen.

Angela sat at the island, enjoying her coffee. The kids were nowhere in sight—probably upstairs getting ready for Jerome to pick them up.

"You're looking positively perky," her sister remarked as Megan got her cup and filled it.

She turned, leaned on the counter, shrugged and sipped.

"Oh, keeping secrets, are we?" Angela teased.

"Well…" Megan paused to savor another sip. "I had a date last night. A dream date. With a terrific guy."

"Things are going well, then?"

Megan went over and took the seat beside Angela's. "Give that woman a gold star."

"I have to say, whatever you did with him, you should keep doing it. You are *glowing*."

Megan nudged her sister with her shoulder. "It's not what you think. Not yet, anyway."

She chuckled. "How do you know what I think?"

Megan set down her cup. "Just a wild guess—and I'm going out with him again today."

Angela clucked her tongue. "Staying out till all hours again?"

"Maybe. And just maybe I won't come home at all until morning...." *Gaaaa.* Had she really said that? And was she really ready to spend a night with Greg?

Angela faked a gasp. "Thoroughly shocking." And they both laughed.

As usual, Jerome arrived late. He and the kids didn't head out the door until almost ten-thirty. As soon as they were gone, Angela took off to get groceries.

Megan went up to her place and got her things together and then went down and waited in the main house for the car to arrive. The doorbell rang at 10:45. She shouldered her roomy tote and hustled to the foyer, where she threw open the door, ready with a nice, wide smile for Andy or Jerry or whoever Greg had sent to drive her to his place.

The smile froze on her face.

It was Rhonda Johnson, frizzy red hair smoothed carefully back, wearing a trim-looking summer shift, and cute yellow sandals on her tiny, freckled feet.

"Megan." Rhonda's smile was the smile of a cobra—just before it opens its thin mouth wide and reveals its long, poisonous fangs. "I was hoping I'd catch you."

Chapter Nine

Megan wasn't fooled. Rhonda was much more than *hoping* to catch her. Rhonda and Irene made it their business to know the schedules of everyone in the neighborhood. If either of them wanted to catch you, they always did.

Too bad Rhonda hadn't arrived just a few minutes later. By then, Megan would have escaped—to Manhattan and the wonderful man who waited for her there....

"I've got a little job for you." Rhonda held up a plain sheet of white paper with notes scribbled all over it in a big, bold hand. "May I come in?" It sounded like a question. It wasn't.

Megan knew she should simply tell Rhonda no.

Nothing good was going to come of inviting the woman in. Rhonda had seen her and Greg together, and Megan could tell by the anticipatory gleam in those cool gray eyes that the subject of Greg *would* come up. Rhonda would make sure that it did.

"Well?" she demanded.

Years of getting along and going along took over. Megan stepped to the side.

Rhonda trotted on past her, headed for the family room, where she perched on the sofa, her delicate feet barely touching the floor. "What I've got is a flyer I need some help with. I know you need the business." She patted the space beside her. "Sit right here. I'll tell you what I'm after."

Megan grimly did as she had instructed.

"Now," said Rhonda, holding up her scribbled sheet of paper. "I need a three-fold mailer—you know, the kind where you use the flyer itself as the envelope? Red paper, I think. People tend to notice red. Or purple. Purple would be fine, too. The Rosewood Ladies Auxiliary is putting on their annual rummage sale and—" She sniffed. Delicately. "Why, Megan. Is that perfume?"

"Yes," Megan said with a soft sigh.

"Very nice."

"Thank you."

"Very…sensual." Rhonda let her voice trail off significantly. Then she started in again. "And I like what you're wearing. This vivid teal is wonderful on you, though teal works well with almost any coloring. The cut is good, too. So…slimming." She frowned, as if something had just occurred to her. "Are you going somewhere?"

Megan sat a little a straighter. "Well, as a matter of fact, yes, I am. I'm going into the city for the day."

"Shopping?"

She told the truth—"I have a date"—and instantly wished that she hadn't.

"Oh. How sweet." And the cobra struck. "With Carly's husband?"

Megan took a slow breath. Her heart was knocking hard against her breastbone. She felt kind of sick to her stomach, too. She simply didn't do conflict well. Not at home. Never at home....

All at once, she was a child again. A child of eight. Or nine. Or ten. A child who'd lost her parents and her annoying little brother. A child who only wanted someone to love her, to accept her, to let her stay with them....

Megan shut her eyes and shook her head. Reminded herself that she was a grown woman now, that those lonely years were well behind her.

Somehow she managed to speak slowly and clearly. "Maybe you hadn't heard. Carly is divorced."

Rhonda waved a slim, freckled hand. "Oh, yes. I heard. But everyone in the neighborhood knows she's been hoping and praying that Greg will see the light and come back to her. I'm sure *you* know it. I mean, given that Carly considers you her *friend*."

Megan wondered what awful things Carly might have said to Rhonda—and then realized immediately that Carly would have said nothing. No matter how hurt and furious she might be, she would never discuss her private life with Rhonda Johnson.

This was just business as usual. Rhonda had seen Carly with Greg and instantly jumped to her own conclusions.

"People are talking," Rhonda said primly. She actually reached over and patted Megan's hand. Her touch was cool and smooth as the white belly of a poisonous snake. "I can't say I agree with your actions. But if you need someone to confide in... I'm here, Megan. You can tell me. Everything. I'll do my best to lend a friendly ear and keep an open mind about—"

It was too much. Way over the line. Even for Megan, who was willing to put up with a lot to keep the peace on Danbury Way. She jumped to her feet. "Um. No." She heard herself add, "Thank you," and despised herself for her own inability to confront trouble on her home turf.

Rhonda peered up at her, disapproval evident in every inch of her itsy-bitsy body. "Well. If that's how you feel."

"It is." The doorbell rang. "And that's my ride. I have to go."

Twin lines had formed between Rhonda's red brows. "But I haven't finished telling you what I want for the flyer."

Megan gulped. "You know what? I've got a packed work schedule. I'm afraid I just won't have time to do this one."

Rhonda blinked. "But it's for the Ladies Auxiliary. An excellent cause. We need you to—"

"Sorry. Can't." Megan backed toward the foyer and the front door. "And I really do have to go now…."

At last, Rhonda slid her little bitty feet to the floor and stood. "Well. All right then," she huffed. "I guess I'll have to scramble around trying to find someone else to do the flyer at the last minute. But what do you care? You're just too busy."

Megan said nothing. She'd only be stuttering out disgusting apologies, anyway. And why add fuel to Rhonda's self-righteous fire?

Rhonda flounced past her, headed for the foyer, leaving Megan to trail along behind her, feeling sick at heart and hating herself for caring so much that Rhonda would be spreading ugly rumors about her. The little redhead reached the door and flung it wide—to find Greg on the doorstep, looking heartbreaker-handsome in khakis and a polo shirt.

Oh, Lord. He'd never mentioned he was coming to pick her up in person.

"Well," said Rhonda, snide as they come. "Look who's here."

Greg got the picture. There was no way he could miss it. He said, carefully, "Hello, Rhonda."

The woman didn't bother to reply. She just pinched up her mouth and strutted off down the steps. Megan and Greg watched her go. Neither of them moved or spoke until she disappeared from view.

Finally, Greg asked, "What the hell was that?"

"You don't even want to know." The limo waited at the curb for them, Jerry behind the wheel. "I'll get my stuff and we can—"

But Greg already had her by the shoulders. He walked her backward through the open door. Once they were in, he guided the door shut with his heel. Those deep brown eyes probed hers. "You're white as a sheet. And you're shaking…."

"No…"

"Yeah."

She admitted, "Rhonda dropped by to ask me to design a rummage sale flyer—or so she said. She *really* came to beat me up for stealing you from Carly."

He swore under his breath. "You didn't *steal* me from anybody. Not that it's any business of Rhonda Johnson's, either way."

"Tell that to Rhonda. I doubt she'll listen."

"Hey. Come here…." He pulled Megan against him. She stiffened at first, resisting his offer of comfort. But his warm arms felt so good—so cherishing—around her. After a moment, with a small, sad sigh, she cuddled in close.

Greg kissed the crown of her head and whispered, "Don't worry about Rhonda. She's a bitch with way too much time on her hands."

Megan tipped her head up to him. "You're right. And I know it. But she gets to me, anyway."

He kissed the tip of her nose. "What can I do? Anything. You name it."

"There's nothing anyone can do about Rhonda."

"You'd be surprised. I might…kidnap that yippy little dog of hers. Hold it for ransom. Not give it back until Rhonda swears never to gossip again."

Megan arched a brow. "You want a dog?"

"Rhonda's dog? Hell, no."

"Well, if you try that, you'll *have* Rhonda's dog. Because Rhonda will never stop gossiping. Not even to get her Yorkie back."

"I could have her banned from Banning's."

Megan faked an awestruck expression. "Including the post-holiday sale?"

"Yeah. Even that."

She still had to shake her head. "I'm afraid even being blackballed from Banning's wouldn't make Rhonda Johnson keep her mouth shut."

"The woman is sick."

"No argument there."

Greg kissed Megan, a quick one. "And you're smiling. At last."

"What do you know? I guess I am…." She lifted her mouth to him and slid her arms up around his neck. He took the hint and kissed her again—a long, sweet one that time, the very best kind.

When they finally came up for air, he asked after Angela and the kids. Megan explained that the kids had gone with their father, and Angela was off at Rosewood Market doing the weekly shopping.

"I'll say hi next time, then." *Next time.* Now, that did sound lovely. He added, "You ready?"

"I'll get my things…."

* * *

They went shopping. At Banning's.

When Jerry dropped them off in front of the store, Megan teased, "A man who likes to shop. Is there such an animal?"

Greg grunted. "It's doubtful. I may run a department store chain, but I hate to shop as much as the next guy. There does come a time, though, when shopping is unavoidable. And this is it."

"Sounds grim."

"Let's get it over with." He led her through the glass doors, past the perfume and makeup counters, through women's sportswear and into the big home furnishings section at the rear.

A guy in a well-cut blue suit came running. His name tag said he was the department manager. "Mr. Banning. So good to see you again…."

Greg nodded. "Ted. This is Megan." The manager beamed her a thousand-watt smile. "Furniture," Greg said. "We need a houseful. Three bedroom sets, dining room table and breakfast nook. And the works for the main living room."

Megan caught on. "Your house. In Rosewood…"

He looked so pleased with himself. "Well, you did point out that it was empty. I've decided it's time to do something about that."

Ted suggested gleefully, "Let's start with the living room, shall we? Right this way…."

It took them a couple of hours to settle on all the pieces. Greg kept insisting he needed Megan's opinion, and she constantly reminded him, "It's your house. You're the one who has to live with what you choose."

"Help," he said, and tried to look really pitiful.

So she would make suggestions based on the house as she remembered it, choosing pieces she thought would go well in the large, comfortable rooms. A lot of neutrals, with occasional bright accent pieces, everything with clean, simple lines.

He would say, "That's good. I really like that," to just about every suggestion she made.

Ted, beaming the whole time, agreed with her choices, as well.

When they had what Greg needed to furnish each room, he paid the huge invoice without batting an eye, and told Ted where to have it all delivered. "Call me at the office," he said. "I'll be sure someone's there to let the delivery crew in."

"Absolutely, Mr. Banning. You can count on me."

They went to major appliances. Megan helped Greg decide on a washer and dryer combination.

From there, they went to housewares, where, once again, Greg had her doing the choosing for him. She picked out good china and everyday dishes, flatware and silver, glassware and crystal. Not to mention a huge array of chef-quality cookware and kitchen gadgets, utensils and small appliances.

When the housewares saleslady added everything up and Megan saw the total, she stifled a gasp—and then teased Greg that he would end up broke if he didn't watch himself.

"Hey. I'm getting the employee discount." And he whipped out his platinum card and passed it to the saleslady, who was beaming every bit as widely as the guy in the furniture department had done.

Megan watched Greg as he signed on the dotted line. He told the salesclerk that he'd already bought furniture and he would be buying towels and bedding and whatever else he could think of that he might need in his new house. He wanted everything sent to the Rosewood address.

"Coordinate with Ted in home furnishings and Marlene in major appliances. I want it all brought up to Rosewood at the same time."

The housewares lady bobbed her head eagerly. Anything for Mr. Banning....

Megan wondered what it would be like, being Greg Banning. Your every wish someone else's command. To her, it seemed magical and glamorous: a limo always waiting to take him wherever he wanted to go, salespeople eager to see that he got exactly what he wanted.

And women...

Well, there must be women, mustn't there? Other women than Megan, that is—and Carly.

Megan thought of her former friend with the usual twinge of guilt. Was Carly doing all right? Megan did hope so....

And then Greg glanced over and smiled at her, and she pushed the guilty thoughts away. He was, truly, a prince of a guy. And Megan couldn't help but notice the way other women—gorgeous, sophisticated-looking women—noticed *him.* So far today, right there in Banning's, Megan had spotted more than one striking woman who had glanced at him—and looked again.

Like when they'd first entered the store. A stunning brunette had paused in midstride at the sight of him, her fawnlike gaze lingering on his broad shoulders, his movie-star-handsome face. And what about that petite blonde with the sexy, spiky hair behind the cosmetics counter? She'd tried so hard to catch his eye—and when he didn't even glance her way, she'd ended up frowning at Megan with a truly unflattering mixture of puzzlement and disbelief.

And what about the gorgeous Asian woman in home furnishings? She'd lingered nearby as Megan helped Greg choose those three bedroom sets, pretending to study the various floor displays, but actually waiting for him to look over and see her standing there.

He hadn't—not that Megan could tell, anyway.

So strange. He seemed totally unaware of all the beautiful women who wanted him to glance their way. But when it came to Megan, he behaved as if he couldn't take his eyes off of her.

It was…kind of dizzying, really. To have a guy like Greg so interested in her. Heady and exciting and just a little bit unreal. She kept thinking she should pinch herself, to make sure she wasn't dreaming.

And that made her want to laugh out loud. After

all, as she'd told him yesterday, if he wanted to adore her, he should go right on ahead.

"Are you hungry?" he asked as they left the housewares department. It was after four.

"Starved. Let's eat."

They had hot dogs from a street vendor, Jerry in the limo trailing them as they strolled along 34th Street, laughing and chatting, discussing how Greg's new furniture ought to be arranged in each room, eating their lovely, late, junk-food lunch.

Then came more shopping. They stopped in at Macy's.

Greg teasingly threatened, "Don't ever tell anyone at Banning's I was here."

"Never," Megan vowed.

They bought Egyptian cotton towels and linens for the master bedroom in a really nice sage-green and gray—and then moved on to Bloomingdales, where he picked up some lamps and a couple of occasional tables for the entryway. From Bloomies they went on to Saks.

Finally, they returned to Banning's, where she made *him* do some choosing—of various vases and mirrors and other decorative touches.

It was after eight when they finally called it quits. They went to a quiet little place in the Village for a leisurely dinner. They talked about anything and everything. He told her more about growing up a Banning, and she elaborated on her plans for Design Solutions.

At a little before eleven, they emerged onto the

darkened Greenwich Village street. Jerry was right there waiting, with the limo.

Greg pulled her close beneath the streetlamp for a quick, sweet kiss. Then he told Jerry, "Take us to the apartment," and a naughty little thrill went shivering through her. Greg sent her a warm glance. "Okay with you?" She nodded. He kissed her again. "Good."

In the plush comfort of the car, when he reached for her hand, she twined her fingers with his. By then, to Megan, the night ahead seemed meant to be— *their* night. Together. In the most intimate way. At last.

The limo glided to a stop at the curb. Jerry held the door for them and they got out. Megan waited, a tingle of anticipation making her feel all shivery inside, as Greg paid the driver and sent him on his way.

In the apartment, Greg offered wine. She accepted. They kicked off their shoes and sat on that gorgeous Italian leather couch of his, in the moody, shadowed light provided by the single lamp he'd lit.

He touched his glass to hers. "To a good day. The best. You. Me…"

"And your platinum credit card."

He leaned closer for a brushing kiss. "Admit it. You like a man with a big…wallet."

She sipped her wine. It was excellent. "A big wallet is nice. But first and foremost, a man should have a sense of humor."

"You women always say that."

"Because it's true."

"What else—after the sense of humor?"

"He should be a good kisser. Definitely."

He kissed her again. "I'm working on it."

"Truth is, you started out fabulous and you only got better from there."

"Now, that's what I like to hear."

"Not that I'm exactly an expert…" In fact, she was so far from being an expert on kissing, it was laughable.

He caught her chin as she tried to look away. "Hey. Whatever it is, you can say it. You can say anything to me."

Crazy. She believed him. And she told him, "Women look at you. All the time. Beautiful women. You have to know that."

He shrugged. "So? Men look at you."

"Oh, come on."

But he was insistent. "They do. Believe me, I notice. But you don't see it. You're oblivious to how…*alive* you are, how downright gorgeous. How sexy, how *real*…"

She laughed and put up a hand. "Stop. All this flattery will go to my head."

"It's not flattery. It's the truth."

She teased, "You're only trying to get me into bed."

He arched a brow. "Well, there is that."

She touched his cheek with the side of her hand. Slow heat trickled through her. And she told him the truth, in a breath-held whisper. "I…want that, too—to spend the night here. With you."

"Megan. Damn. I was hoping you'd say that." He took her chin again and he kissed her, a brushing, lovely, soft kiss—a series of them, really, back and forth across her eager lips, setting off sparks and heat and that wonderful, warm, melting feeling down below. When he pulled away, he sat back far enough to sip more wine and look at her as if she were the most fabulous woman in the whole of the five boroughs and beyond.

She gulped and ordered her racing heart to slow down a little. "I think it's only fair to warn you...."

He caught a lock of her hair, rubbed it between his fingers. "Go ahead. Hit me with it. I can take it, whatever it is."

"You, um, say that you think I'm sexy."

"Because you are."

"Maybe. But I'm not very...experienced."

His mouth kicked up on one side. "Exactly how inexperienced are you?"

"Well, I'm not a virgin."

He smiled a little wider. "Whew. Had me worried there...."

"Oh, very funny."

His expression was instantly serious. "Listen."

"What?"

"It doesn't matter. It's not how experienced you are—or aren't. It's *you,* Megan. I just want you."

His words helped. A lot. They made a glow—in her heart, all through her. She touched his face again, traced that nose that would have looked just right on a Roman coin, caressed his slightly stubbled cheek and each of his sable brows.

He kissed her fingertips as they brushed his mouth. "Say it," he commanded. "If you're afraid whatever it is that you're thinking is going to sound strange or silly…it's not. Just tell me."

She groaned. "Oh, all right. The truth is, you're the first guy I've even *kissed* since college. How odd is that?"

"Not odd," he whispered. "Not odd in the least…."

She released the breath she hadn't even realized she'd been holding. "Well, I have to say, it's nice to hear you tell me that."

He set his wine on the coffee table and she set hers beside it. And then he reached for her, stretching out on the sofa, pulling her down so she rested half on the sofa and half on top of him. Once he had her arranged to his satisfaction, he threaded his fingers up into her hair and combed down the length of the strands in a lazy, slow stroke.

"So tell me about the guy in college." He smoothed her hair so it fanned out on her shoulders.

"Oh, puh-leese." She folded her hands on his chest and rested her chin on them.

"I'm serious. I think I'm jealous."

"Why? You have absolutely no need to be."

"Say that again."

"All right, if you insist. Don't be jealous. There's no reason."

"Good to hear—and tell me about him anyway."

Greg ran a slow finger down the side of her neck. "Come on…"

"Oh, all right. His name was Seth Prankmier…"

"Let me guess—he looked just like Brad Pitt, right?"

"Not even close. He was studying to be a painter."

"Ah. The artistic type."

"Seth weighed maybe one-ten soaking wet and he wore a long scarf and a black beret and he quoted famous poets. Only the dead ones. As I remember, I met him at a poetry reading…."

"And you kissed him?"

"I did. I also slept with him—and don't you dare ask me to tell you about *that.* All I'm going to say is that it was more than once and maybe it shouldn't have been. I kept hoping it would get better, you know?"

"Not a match, huh? You and Seth?"

"Right. Very, very not a match. Now, what about you?"

He pretended to look innocent. "What do you mean, me?"

And she realized she didn't really want to know how many model-thin, drop-dead-beautiful women he had slept with. "You know what? Never mind. Don't tell me."

He said, "The truth is, there have been a few. Before I was married. And after."

"What about during?"

He looked directly into her eyes. "Never. I was true to my wife. To my marriage."

Megan realized she'd been holding her breath again, and let it out on a relieved sigh. "I believe you were. And I'm glad."

He caught her by the shoulders and urged her up until her mouth hovered above his. "No one," he whispered, his breath warm against her lips.

She frowned, not following. "No one?"

"...like you, Megan. No one ever like you...."

"Oh, Greg...."

"It all starts with a kiss," he whispered. "You should do that now."

So she did; she lowered her mouth to cover his.

Chapter Ten

He undressed her right there, in the living area, in the glow of the city lights beyond the windows.

At first, she was so scared—that he'd see her not-concave tummy and her too-full thighs and find her suddenly less attractive, even regret that he had charmed her and pursued her until they came to this moment: here, in the moonlight, the two of them, alone, shedding the final protection of their clothes.

But he only whispered, once and then again and again, that she was beautiful, as he revealed every inch of her—full breasts, round belly and curving hips. He pulled her to her feet and he looked at her, long and slowly, his gaze sweeping from her flushed face to her pink-painted toenails and back up to meet her waiting eyes again.

He said it once more: "Beautiful…" And he reached out, brushing his open palm against her breast, causing the nipple to draw up tight in excitement. And yearning. "So beautiful…."

She believed him. How could she not? She saw the truth in his dark, soft eyes. He looked at her and saw her beauty.

She wasn't perfect—but then, he'd told her from the first that he'd never wanted perfect. Greg wanted *her*. He wanted her just as she was. He truly did. And that made the constricting grip of her fear ease to a shadow and fall away to nothing. Her fear, after all, was only one more unneeded covering, one more barrier between them.

And all barriers must fall….

She whispered his name as she stepped up close, granting him a quick kiss, taking the sides of his polo shirt and skimming it upward. He raised his arms for her and she whipped it off and away.

Talk about beautiful….

His chest was hard, the muscles clearly cut, his skin silvered in the moonlight. "Oh, Greg…." She rested both hands against his heart, felt his heartbeat, like a promise, so deep and strong and sure.

He pulled her close and took her mouth and…

Oh, there was nothing like it. Greg's strong arms around her, his big chest against her soft breasts, his heart beating in time to hers. He kissed her and he kissed her some more, his skilled tongue finding all the wet, secret hollows beyond her lips—finding them, stroking them, exciting her so that her whole body seemed to shimmer. Between her legs, she yearned and opened—wet. And so very needful.

He stroked a burning caress—down her arm, back up again, along her side, over the wide-flaring curve of her hip…and inward.

She gasped and then cried out.

And he did what he always did—smiled against her mouth in that special, tender, knowing way of his as his fingers combed the tight curls and then smoothly delved, parting her, sliding along the slick, sensitive inner lips, finding that special spot where her pleasure was greatest. He caressed that spot and she cried out again.

He muttered her name and he went on touching her there. She rocked against him, already spinning beyond herself, out of control in the most exquisite, unbearable, amazing way. He eased a finger inside—two—all the while using his thumb on that secret, swollen bud.

The world, spinning so fast now and glittering wildly, tightened down to that one spot—and then exploded. Pleasure claimed her, washing over her in pulsing waves. She clutched his shoulders, buried her head in the warm, firm curve of his neck and held on for dear life.

The pleasure crested and cascaded outward so that she saw a million shooting stars, each one popping and flashing on the dark screen of her shut eyelids. Finally, slowly, the wonder faded to a shimmer and then to a soft echo, leaving her weak and sighing, clinging to him for support, thinking how she could hardly move.

He gathered her closer, wrapping both arms around her, nuzzling her hair, nipping her ear with tender little biting kisses, kisses that teased and thrilled and made her feel every bit as beautiful as he'd told her she was.

"Ohmygolly…" She made a sound that was both a moan and a giggle at once.

He chuckled. "Say that again."

She looked up at him. "Let me elaborate. Wow and double wow."

He bent to nip her ear once more. She shivered in delight. He whispered, "Time for bed, I think."

"Oh, well sure. Easy for you to say. If I let go of you, I'll only fall over."

"No problem." Effortlessly, he bent and scooped her up against his bare chest.

She laughed in sheer joy as he lifted her high. "If you drop me, I will kill you."

"Megan," he said reproachfully, "don't you know yet that you can count on me?"

She wrapped her arms around his shoulders, pressed her lips to his neck and whispered happily, "I'm learning. Believe me. I honestly am…."

His platform bed was acres wide. He laid her down on it with infinite care. And then he stepped back to skim off his khakis and the checked silk boxers beneath.

When he stood up again, the sight of him stunned her—stole her breath and made her heart do something totally impossible beneath her ribs. He had one of those stomachs you could scrub your laundry on. And narrow, hard hips. And big, hard thighs.

And from the tangled nest of dark hair where those thighs came together, his erection jutted out at her. Very big. And very ready.

"Oh, Greg. You are something to look at," she told him in an awestruck whisper.

His eyes holding hers, he opened the drawer in the night table beside the bed and brought out a condom, setting it on top, ready for the moment when it would be needed. Then, at last, he came down to join her, pulling her to him, tucking her head under his chin and stroking her hair as if he treasured her above everything and everyone in the whole wide world.

His big, warm hand swept down to the small of her back and he pressed her in, closer still, to his heat and maleness. The warmth in her midsection bloomed into flame as she felt him, so hard and thick, nudging her stomach, rubbing her down low. She moaned and lifted her mouth for yet another of those endless, seeking kisses.

Oh, there was nothing—nothing like his kiss. He kissed her and his hands explored her, stroking up and down the curve of her back, over the generous swell of her bottom, up again to learn the rounded shape of her shoulders, then slipping between them to cup each full breast.

And her mouth wasn't all he kissed. Oh, my, no. Those warm, soft lips of his went roaming, over her chin, down the line of her throat, which she stretched for him with a long, low moan. He licked the twin points of her collarbones, dipped into the soft hollow between them.

And went lower.

Capturing one aching, taut nipple, he sucked, slowly, circling the areole with his so-clever tongue, then sucking harder.

Deeper....

Megan gave herself up to his skill and his tenderness, clutching the silk spread, tossing her head on the pillows, so that her hair came alive, crackling with static, clinging to the silk as she moaned out her excitement, her willingness, her need....

He trailed more kisses down between her breasts, around her belly button, over the curve of her abdomen and then into the curls that covered her mound.

She gasped in delight as he kissed her some more, parting her with his tongue, stunning her with his wet, rough-velvet caress, so that she cried out his name and begged him to fill her.

"Not yet," he whispered. "Not yet..."

With his mouth, he found that special spot. He licked it and teased it, even caught it so very gently between his strong teeth, and flicked it, maddeningly, with his naughty tongue.

By then she was writhing beneath him, making low, urgent, pleading sounds. Again she felt her body rising, gathering to hit the peak once more. She moaned and she pleaded in a breathless, yearning whisper, "Oh, Greg. Now. Please, please…now…"

And still he kissed her in that secret, most intimate way, until she could hold back no longer and the waves of sensation took her, rolling over her, spinning all through her, tossing her to the edge and beyond—out into a boundless universe studded with stars.

Greg felt the tiny, hot pulsing, tasted the silky spill of greater wetness when she hit the peak. He stayed with her, kissing her, drawing it out, making it last….

She was so sweet and so sexy—and yet innocent, too. Eager and amazingly responsive. But tight.

She'd said she hadn't had a lover since that poet in college—and the poet had hardly counted, from the way she'd described how it had been with him.

Greg had to remember that. He had to go slow with her. Had to make it good for her. He didn't want to hurt her. He wanted to be certain she was truly ready to take him.

So he continued his intimate kiss, until the tiny contractions faded down to almost nothing, until she sighed, her pretty, curvy body going limp, her soft arms thrown wide.

It was then, when she went boneless and loose, that he knew it was time. At last….

He lifted his head, lowering it again to press one last, gentle kiss on the tight, shiny curls that covered her sex. She panted, lifting up a little, staring down at him through glazed eyes.

"Oh, Greg…" Words seemed to fail her. She let her head drop back down.

He got up on his knees and reached for the condom, slipping it free of its wrapping, rolling it smoothly down over his aching erection. When he glanced at her sweet, flushed face again, he saw she was watching him now, her eyes wide, her sweet mouth swollen and lax from pleasure and kisses. With a small moan, she lifted both arms, reaching for him.

And he went down to her, bracing his upper body on his hands as he settled his hips between her thighs, nudging them wider with one knee and then the other, positioning himself. She moaned his name again, reaching down, closing her hand around him.

He threw his head back with a hard groan, almost losing it right then. "Careful," he warned her, the sound guttural, rough with his straining effort at self-control.

She smiled a tiny, womanly smile and stroked him, slow strokes, up and down the shaft, careful of the condom, but with such tender and purposeful concentration. Each stroke brought intense pleasure—a pleasure very close to pain. He shut his eyes and he bore it. She was killing him. It felt so good.

As she stroked, she eased his way in, her body opening to him, warm and wet and so welcoming….

Finally, when she held him within her, she reached up, tipping her mouth to him, pulling him down along the soft, willing length of her. He kissed her, slow and deep, and then, as the pleasure grew yet more achingly intense, he buried his head in the curve of her shoulder. Through gritted teeth, he warned, "I can't…hold back…."

Her hands stroked his spine, straying lower. She surged up against him and pulled him tight to her at the same time. He groaned as he slid in that tiny bit deeper, as he felt her firm, satiny inner muscles tighten around him, then loosen, stroking him, arousing him even more than before.

If that was possible….

"Don't, then," she whispered. "Don't hold back…."

"I don't want…to hurt you."

"You won't. You can't…."

And by then, it was too much: the feel of her all around him, her soft hands stroking his back, her full breasts against his chest, the sweet, clean scent of her skin….

He began to move, a slow glide at first. She wrapped her legs around him and went with him, her body instantly picking up the rhythm from his.

Careful. He really needed to be careful. And he tried, tried so hard….

But she was so eager, so open, so willing. And he did want all of her—to be buried to the hilt in her curvy, soft body; to feel those tender arms around him, her heels pressing into him, urging him on.

Everything flew away. He moved wildly and she went with him. He heard his own low, pleasured groans and her tender, encouraging cries and moans.

Faster.

Harder.

He was out of control and he knew it. It was good and it was right....

Had never been so right before.

He threw back his head at the end and he called her name—out loud that time.

She whispered, "Greg," and he was going over, pushing so hard into her, feeling her body contracting around him, her climax catching fire from his.

The hot pulsing started, burning along his every nerve, emptying him out in a release that never seemed to end.

Finally, after forever, he went limp and heavy on top of her, crushing her, though he knew he shouldn't.

She didn't seem to mind in the least. She only stroked his back and kissed him and whispered with a sweet, low chuckle, "Oh, my, my—or did I say that before?"

In time, they left the bed, poured themselves more wine and went to soak in the big tub he'd had installed when he bought the loft. He turned on the massage jets. She laughed and lay back in his arms, and he found himself wishing he could hold her there, with him, that he would never have to let her go.

He whispered, only half teasing, "Sorry, but I think you'll just have to stay here forever."

Beneath the water, she ran her finger up his thigh. He knew she could feel him, at her back, growing harder again. She gave a husky laugh. "Forever, huh?"

He nuzzled her hair, which curled into charming little corkscrews in the steam that drifted up from the tub. "Didn't I just say that?"

"Oh, yeah. You did."

He shifted, leaning farther back, pulling her with him, so they were floating together, loose and easy in the hot, bubbling water, her body above his. "That's right. You'll have to stay. There's no escaping. I've decided to make you my sex slave."

She let her arms float out, trailed them on top of the bubbling water. "Hmm. A sex slave. What's the pay like?"

He told her sternly, "Slaves don't get paid."

"Well, then. I guess I would have to focus on enjoying my work."

"An excellent attitude." He nuzzled her hair. "And if you please me, there could be…benefits."

"Full medical, you mean? A retirement plan?"

He took her soft shoulders, floated her up a little, until he could kiss that smooth, steam-wet throat of hers. Obligingly, she tipped her head to the side to give him easier access. He nipped where he kissed. She made a small, pleasured sound. He said, "Anything is possible."

Lazily, she rolled until she was facing him, her breasts lightly touching his chest, the curls between her thighs brushing that part of him that was rock-hard all over again. "I'm nuts for you," she said, and floated up to kiss his lips.

"Nuts is good," he told her decisively, when she drifted slightly away again. Her expression changed, a slight frown taking form between her brows, her mouth tightening a fraction. He commanded, "Whatever it is, tell me…."

"Oh, it's nothing…."

He didn't believe her. "It's something." Under the water, he touched her breast. She gasped. And he touched her lower—much lower, parting the weightless, floating curls and pressing a finger at her most sensitive spot. When she gasped again, he repeated, "Tell me."

She tried to look firm. "Not when you're touching me like that. I can't think when you do that."

Reluctantly, he took his hand away. "Now. Tell me."

She floated away—and he let her. She seemed to need the distance right then. At the other end of the tub, she turned, leaned back against the marble rim and faced him. "When you still lived in the neighborhood, before your breakup with Carly…" The words lost momentum. She fell silent, her sweet face pink—with the heat of the water? Or something else?

He nudged her knee. "Say it."

She had her arms out to the sides, her hands gripping the tub rim a little too hard. "It's really dumb. And embarrassing. And it also makes me wonder about myself, a little. About my own motives, you know?"

"This doesn't sound the least bit dumb to me. It sounds like something you really want to tell me."

"Oh, Greg…" She seemed to lose her nerve. And then she sucked in a big breath and blurted, "I had a crush on you. I did. Even though you were married, even though whenever you looked at me, you looked right through me, still. I used to…" She bit her lower lip. "Oh, this is too dumb…." She wandered off into silence again, her eyes shifting away.

Greg waited. He knew her well enough already to know that there were times when she needed stumble around a little, to find her own way to wherever she was going.

"Okay," she said bleakly at last. "It was like this. You hardly realized I existed, but I was always fantasizing what it might be like, if you weren't married…. If by some miracle you would notice me…"

He understood then. "Megan. It's not your fault that Carly and I broke up. Not your fault by any stretch of a wild imagination. You had nothing to do with any of that."

"Oh, I know. I know I didn't. But I did lie to myself, when Carly said she'd get me that interview with you. I told myself the crush I had on you was long over. But then, the minute I saw you, sitting behind that big glass desk of yours…"

He said it again. "Not your fault."

She was shaking her head. "See, though. If I had been honest with myself—"

"What? You would have told Carly no thank you,

turned down a major opportunity for Design Solutions, because of the possibility that you and I might end up right where we are now?"

She thought about that, chewing her lip some more, looking conflicted and very cute, with the tops of her creamy breasts showing above the water and her hair a wild tangle of curls, drops of water caught in it, twinkling like diamonds. "Okay," she said at last.

"Okay, what?"

"I would have told myself that it didn't matter if I had a crush on you, because you'd never shown any interest in me and there was no reason to believe you suddenly would."

"And you would have come to the interview."

"Right."

He lifted his hand from the water and held it out to her. She hesitated only a fraction of a second before laying her fingers in his. Once he had hold of her, he sat a little higher in the tub and reeled her in, turning her so that she was tucked against his chest as before. He smoothed her wild hair aside and kissed her ear. "Stop beating yourself up. That's an order."

"Yes, Master."

"I like the way you say that." He cupped her breasts. They were so gorgeous. He loved the way they filled his hands. She gave a tiny little moan and let her head fall back on his shoulder. Her hair trailed, clinging to his chest, floating on the water, foaming out around them.

He rolled her nipples and scraped his teeth lightly

along the moist, sweet, peach-scented flesh of her neck. "Moan like that again," he whispered.

And she did. Repeatedly.

When morning light came pouring in the tall windows, Megan rolled her head on the pillow to find Greg right there beside her, awake already, watching her.

He guided a hank of hair out her eyes. "You look so trusting when you're sleeping."

She curled on her side facing him and reached out to stroke a slow hand down the muscular shape of his arm. He was so warm. Brown-gold hairs dusted his forearm. "It was…all real, wasn't it? Last night, I mean…."

"Oh, yeah."

"Better than my wildest fantasies…." She couldn't help giggling. "Well, okay. The truth is, my fantasies weren't all that wild." She blew out a big, fake sigh. "Lack of experience. It's a terrible thing."

"You were amazing," he said. And she knew he meant it.

He drew her to him, cradled her in those big arms. The sheet slipped down. They made love again in the bright light of morning. Megan lost herself in the heat and the wonder of it.

Later, she wrapped herself in Greg's terry-cloth robe and he pulled on an old pair of sweatpants. They went to the kitchen to scare up a little breakfast.

He had eggs and half a loaf of bread—and coffee, which he ground fresh and put on to brew. They worked together. He made the toast, she scrambled the eggs. They were just sitting down to eat when the downstairs intercom started buzzing.

Greg sent her a wry grin, but stayed in his chair. The intercom buzzed again. She gave him a look. He shrugged. "I was thinking maybe I'd just ignore it. Whoever it is wasn't invited."

Then the phone—the land line on the counter— rang. Greg threw up both hands. "Fine, fine." He pushed back his chair and went to pick it up. "Hello." He listened. He didn't look particularly happy to hear from whoever was on the other end. He dropped into his chair again, sent Megan a quick glance and a shake of his head. Definitely not happy with whoever was calling.

Carly, she thought, her heart sinking. *Please, please don't let it be Carly.*

"Sorry," he said into the phone, sounding much more irritated than regretful. "You never said you were coming by this morning…. Hold on." He punched the mute button. "It's my mother," he said grimly. *Not Carly,* Megan thought. *Good.*

"She's downstairs and she wants to come up."

"Come up? Now?" Megan hadn't reached the point where she'd even considered meeting Vanessa Banning. And if she *had* considered such a meeting, she would never in a million years have chosen for it to happen when she was sitting at Greg's break- fast table, wearing his robe—and nothing else.

"I'll get rid of her."

"Wait…"

He scowled. "There's no reason we have to deal with her right now."

Megan swallowed. Hard. "Yes, there is. She's your mother. It's rude to just send her away."

He let out a humorless laugh. "Sometimes, with my mother, you have to be rude. Otherwise, she'll roll right over you. And she can't expect to show up out of nowhere and be welcomed with open arms."

"Of course she can. She's your mother, Greg."

"I promise you. She's not like any mother *you've* ever known."

Megan popped to her feet. "Just see if you can stall her for a minute or two. Give me time to get dressed. And would you…put on a shirt, maybe?"

He looked at her, frowning. Finally, he nodded. "All right. If you're sure…."

She wasn't. But still, she turned toward the living area and started snatching up her scattered clothes.

Chapter Eleven

Greg was right.

Megan had never seen a mother quite like Vanessa Banning. She was tall and willow-slim, with gleaming, chin-length auburn hair and amazing, totally wrinklefree, translucent skin. She wore a simple cream-colored linen dress. And pearls—a single, perfect strand. She had the grace and assurance of a woman born to privilege, a woman utterly at ease in her rightful place at the top of the society food chain.

She came breezing in with a charming smile. "Well, and here I am." She turned her smile on Megan, who had thrown on yesterday's wrinkled clothes, wore no makeup and knew she looked like just what she was: the woman who'd been making wild love with Vanessa's only son all night long. "And this is…?"

Greg made the introductions. "Megan. My mother, Vanessa. Mother, Megan Schumacher."

"How lovely…" Vanessa extended a smooth, perfectly manicured hand. Megan took it and found it cool as marble. "…to meet you."

Greg said, "Coffee?"

Vanessa gave a regal nod. "I'd adore a cup."

Megan let go of that cold, smooth hand. "Are you hungry? We can whip up some—"

"No." Vanessa waved the pale hand that Megan had just released. "Thank you so much, but just the coffee. Black."

Greg poured his mother a cup and they all three sat at the table. "So, Mother," he said, looking kind of weary all of a sudden. "I thought you were up at the Montauk house." He explained to Megan, "My mother spends her summers in the Hamptons."

"Ah," said Megan, just to say something.

Greg asked Vanessa, "What brings you to town on a Sunday morning?"

"Oh, nothing special. Your father's in Boston. I came in yesterday to do a little shopping. And this morning, well, I thought I'd just drop by and see how you're doing."

Greg looked—what? Guarded? Disbelieving? Megan didn't get it. Aside from a certain oh-so-well-bred coolness of manner, Vanessa had been perfectly polite, even friendly.

He said, "Doing just fine. Mom." The way he paused before the word *Mom* made it seem like a dig.

"Well, yes," said Vanessa, her charming smile unwavering. "I can see that you are." She sipped her coffee and swiveled her head Megan's way. "Now, Megan. I want to know all about you."

"Mother." The word was a warning.

Vanessa laughed, the sound clear and musical. She waved her graceful hand again. "Darling, don't be a bore. I'm sure Megan doesn't mind answering the basic questions."

Megan spoke up. "I don't. Really. I don't mind at all."

"You see?" Vanessa flashed her son another cool glance. "She doesn't mind. At all."

So Megan attempted to eat her lukewarm eggs and toast as Vanessa plied her with questions. Where had she grown up? Gone to school? Who was her family?

Megan took small bites so she could swallow quickly. She answered every question Vanessa threw at her. When she said she lived in Rosewood, Vanessa arched a perfect brow.

"Amazing. It is such a small world, isn't it? Greg's ex-wife lives in Rosewood. I don't imagine you've met Carly?"

Greg was scowling. "Megan lives on Danbury Way, Mother. A few doors down from Carly. They're neighbors—as I'm reasonably sure you already know."

Vanessa didn't answer him. She went on smiling. She said she'd heard about the new contract Banning's had with Megan's company. "Gregory, Sr., told me all about that. He says you're very talented and we're so lucky to have found you. I understand Greg did that—found you?"

Greg set down his coffee cup. "Mother. Enough. Let Megan eat her breakfast in peace."

Vanessa apologized. "Oh, I'm so sorry. Of course, of course." She leaned a little closer to Megan. "But you know…how a mother is."

Megan nodded. "I understand. I honestly do."

Vanessa started to say something.

But Greg asked, "How was the ride down into the city?"

His mother sent him a look. "Uneventful." Again she turned to Megan, but Greg asked another question before she had time to speak. She answered, brusquely.

And he came right back at her, using her own methods against her, peppering her with an endless raft of questions.

What had she bought during her shopping trip? How was the weather at the shore? Would his father be back in New York on Monday, as planned?

Vanessa answered him each time in as few words as possible: "Various items." "Balmy." "Yes."

She would bite out the answer and start to turn to Megan—and Greg would hit her with another one. This went on for several minutes. Megan watched the exchange. The questions and answers flew back and forth so swiftly, she felt like a spectator at a Ping-Pong match.

At last, Vanessa set down her cup and stood. "Well. I suppose I must be on my way."

"Too bad," said Greg cheerfully—and leaped to his feet to herd her toward the door.

"So nice to meet you, Megan," Vanessa called as he ushered her out of sight into the screened-off entryway.

"Bye," Megan called.

She heard the door open and shut and then Greg reappeared. "She's gone." He made a big show of wiping imaginary sweat from his brow. "Whew."

Megan said, "Oh, come on. She wasn't so bad."

"Because I never let her get rolling."

"Really, Greg, she was kind of nice."

"So was Ted Bundy, from what I hear."

Megan carried their plates to the sink. "I'm serious. She's not that bad."

"You're right. She's not. Carefully controlled. In very small doses. But you have to promise me never to let yourself be alone with her. Not until you and I have been together for at least a decade and there's nothing she can do to tear us apart."

Together for a decade. Of course, he was only teasing. But it did sound good.

"A decade, huh?"

Those dark eyes were gleaming. "That's what I said."

"And what makes you so certain she'd want us apart?"

"Trust me on this."

"But—"

"Tell you what. Let's forget about my mother— at least for today, okay?"

Megan considered for a moment, and decided he had the right idea. Grinning, she snapped her fingers. "Who?"

His smile was slow and oh, so sexy. "Exactly." He came toward her. When he reached her, he cradled her face in his hands and she felt those lovely shivers all through her at the cherishing light in his dark eyes. They kissed. As always, the contact curled her toes and made her sigh in pleasure. When he pulled away, he said, "So what do you want to do today?"

An image of her desk at work popped into her brain—the overflowing in-box, the endless list of stuff that needed doing, ASAP. She pushed that image away. A girl deserved a couple of days off in a row every now and then. Especially if she had someone wonderful to spend them with.

She rested her hands on his chest and beamed up at him. "Let's start with another kiss and take it from there...."

They spent most of the day at the apartment, reading the papers, watching the Sunday political commentaries on CNN and PBS. And of course, making slow, amazing love....

Megan called Angela at three-thirty, just to check in. Angela said that Jerome was due back with the kids at five. "And I'm enjoying an hour and a half of beautiful peace and quiet until then. What about you?"

"I'm having a great time."

"I know you are," Angela said fondly. "I can hear it in your voice."

"And I probably won't be home until late—unless you need me?"

"Nope. Everything's under control."

Megan teased, "Easy to say now—when the kids are away."

"Don't you worry about me. I'm Supermom, remember? Ask anyone in the neighborhood."

Megan told her to call if she changed her mind. And Angela laughed and promised again that she'd be just fine.

At seven that evening, Megan and Greg left the apartment to eat at a restaurant he liked in SoHo. They got back at a little after nine. Megan said that she really had to be getting home.

But then Greg took her in his arms....

At eleven-thirty, he called for a car. And it was midnight when he kissed her good-night on the sidewalk outside the door to his building, as Andy held the limo door wide for her.

She rode home in what could only be called a daze of happiness. Never in her life had she felt so...

Megan giggled, right there in the luxurious silence of the car. She simply could not think of a word fine enough to describe how incredible she felt.

The privacy window slid open. "What was that, Ms. Schumacher?"

"Nothing, Andy." Only pure happiness. Delirious happiness.

"As long as you're all right."

"I am, Andy. I'm very, very all right."

Megan was up in the morning before dawn. She grabbed some coffee and headed for Poughkeepsie, where her in-box was invisible beneath the cascade of mail, where her computer waited, packed with project folders, each one demanding to be dealt with right now.

Greg called at nine. "Working hard?"

"You bet."

"Can you get away tonight?"

Oh, how she wanted to. "I just can't. I've got to go down to Rosewood and watch the kids in the afternoon—and then I've got to get myself back up here. I'll be parked at this desk of mine well after nine tonight."

"You sound frantic."

"I'm not, not really. Just…regretful that I can't take you up on your extremely tempting offer."

"Wednesday night," he said.

"What about it?"

"Can you take Wednesday night off, do you think?"

She shouldn't. But she did long to see him… "Okay. I'll manage it somehow. I do have to watch the kids at four, as usual, though."

"I'll be there."

"'There' meaning?"

"At your sister's place. Say, four-thirty?"

She warned, "Angela won't be home until a

quarter of six or so. It'll be you and me and three little darlings."

"No problem. I'll get some quality time with the kids."

That pleased her, a lot—that he wanted to come early and get to know the kids. Still, she teased him, "Quality time, huh?"

"That's right. And once your sister gets home, you're all mine."

She was blushing, and she knew it. She put her hand against her cheek to cool the fire a little—and right then, Nancy, her assistant, appeared in the door to the hallway and signaled toward the meeting room, where Megan should have been five minutes again. Megan raised her index finger and mouthed, "One minute."

Greg said, "Wednesday. I need a yes."

"Yes. And I have to go…."

When she got home that night, he'd left a message on her apartment line. "It's Greg. I wish it was Wednesday…."

She almost called him. But it was ten forty-five. Even wild, mad lovers needed a little sleep now and then.

Tuesday, he sent flowers to the office—a huge crystal vase of stargazer lilies. She called to thank him. They talked for an hour about nothing in particular. She kept thinking that she really had to go…but somehow, she never did. Finally, he had a meeting he had to get to.

"Tomorrow." He made the word a promise.

"Tomorrow," she echoed, and he was gone.

Again that evening, she returned to the office after Angela came home. Megan worked until ten. And by Wednesday, she was actually beginning to feel more or less on top of her workload.

She could afford to take the night off.

She left the office a little early, so she and the kids would have time to stop at Rosewood Market and still get back home to be there for Greg. They needed milk and eggs and cereal, among other things. With three kids in the house, supplies tended to run low about midweek.

They were barely beyond the market's big sliding doors when Olivia and Michael got into it over which of them would push the cart. Nowadays, the two of them vied for the honor, ever since Michael had decided he was much too grown up to sit in the cart seat—which used to be his favorite thing about shopping.

Not anymore, though. Now, he turned up his nose at the very idea. "That's only for little kids. I want to push. I'm old enough to push. Ask Mom. She lets me."

"He pushed last time," Olivia argued. "And he's too little to do it right, anyway."

"Am not."

"Are so."

Anthony, in headphones with his Game Boy, as always, stood to the side, thumbs flying, eyes fixed on the small screen in his hands, expression rapt.

"Am not!" Michael folded his arms hard over his small chest and stuck out his lower lip.

"Aunt Megan." Olivia stomped her dainty foot. "It's my turn."

"Is not!"

Finally, Megan got them to agree to share. Michael would push to the pasta aisle and Olivia would take over from there. After that, things went relatively smoothly. Megan had Olivia getting stuff off the shelves while Michael pushed—and then, when Olivia's turn came, she enlisted Michael's aid in filling the cart.

They did lose Anthony temporarily in the bread aisle. He forgot to keep up as he reached a new level in his game. But Megan ran back and found him. As always, when she took the kids anywhere, she found herself marveling at her single-mom sis, who managed to do a great job handling all three of them on a day-in, day-out basis. Raising three children, even with a husband to help, was not a task for the faint at heart.

And Greg said he wanted ten kids....

Truly. The man had to be either totally oblivious to the enormity of the job, or joking. She grinned to herself. He'd been exaggerating for effect, and she knew it.

The important thing was, he did want children and so did she. If this magical thing between them went all the way to the altar, she knew they had one important goal in common: kids and all the craziness, challenges and fulfillment the little darlings entailed.

Not that Megan had a clue how she'd handle a family, be an attentive, loving wife *and* deal with all the demands of her growing business. But they'd work it out—well, that is, if it ever came to that: to marriage.

Wow. Talk about a big step. Getting married to Greg. Thinking about it caused a warm glow all through her. A happy, if somewhat nervous glow.

And really, she was getting way ahead of herself here. They weren't anywhere near the altar yet. Why, it had only been a little over two weeks since she'd walked into his office intending to make a purely professional proposal—and quickly discovered that her secret crush wasn't anywhere near as *over* as she'd thought.

Sixteen days since that first meeting. Nine days since their first kiss, in his empty house five blocks from Danbury Way. And four days since Saturday, when they'd made love for the first time—all night long.

Would he be a good husband? She had to face facts here. He'd failed at marriage once—not to mention that the ink was barely dry on his final divorce papers....

And what about her? Really, she was about as inexperienced with men as a twenty-first century girl could get. In her entire twenty-eight years, there'd been Seth Prankmier and now Greg and that was pretty much it....

"Aunt Megan, Aunt Megan!" Megan blinked away her day-dreaming haze. "Look." Olivia, rolling her eyes, pointed at Michael, who was trekking back and forth from one of the freezers, loading the cart with box after box of freezer pops.

"Michael." Megan spoke firmly.

He dropped another box of pops into the cart. "I really like these."

Megan shook her head and patiently explained that two boxes of freezer pops was more than enough, thank you very much. Michael stuck out his lower lip—but he did put the other six boxes of pops back in the freezer where they'd come from.

With Olivia pushing the cart, Michael skipping along beside her and Anthony trailing behind with his Game Boy, Megan turned into the produce aisle—and almost ran smack-dab into Irene Dare, who was blocking the way, chatting with another woman Megan didn't recognize.

"Oops." Irene glanced over, smiling. But when she saw who it was, her eyes narrowed and her thin-lipped mouth drew tight. She nodded, the movement little more than a quick, dismissive jerk of her head. "Megan."

"Hello, Irene." Megan forced a smile—for Irene and for the woman she didn't know—and hurried the kids on by.

One of the best things about Rosewood Market was the demonstrations they always had going in the produce department. A nice lady with a microphone would chop things and make jokes and talk about how to prepare this or that....

Megan tried to enjoy the show the demonstration

lady put on. She helped Michael choose apples and bananas. She did her best to ignore Irene and her friend, who still stood at the corner near the freezers, their heads bent close together. Once, she made the mistake of glancing their way and caught Irene looking straight at her.

Megan knew damn well that Irene was talking about her, spreading stories about her right there in Rosewood Market. She knew it and she hated it. She also knew that Rhonda would be talking about her, too. The knowledge that there had to be gossip going around—featuring Megan as the evil, betraying "other woman"—knotted her stomach and made her heart pound in a heavy, hurtful way. She hustled the kids along and they left the market as quickly as she could manage with three children in tow.

By the time she reached the house, she was feeling a little bit better. The talk would die down. She just needed to give it time—and avoid giving people more to whisper about. Moments like the one Saturday morning, where Rhonda had run into Greg when he came to pick Megan up, had to be avoided at all costs.

It shouldn't be that difficult. As a rule, she and Greg would be meeting in the city, anyway. It wasn't as if they'd be rubbing everyone's noses in their relationship, or anything. For a while, until Rhonda and Irene found someone else to pick on, until Carly had time to accept the end of her marriage and move on, Megan and Greg could kind of keep it low-key, couldn't they? They could be more careful about being seen around town.

Yes. That should work. From now on, whenever possible, *she'd* go to *him*. They'd be together in Manhattan, where people minded their own business.

This evening, they could talk about it. She was certain that he'd understand.

When Greg arrived, about twenty minutes after Megan and the kids got home from the market, she'd managed to put aside her distress at the encounter with Irene. The doorbell rang and she rushed to let him in. She threw back the door and their eyes met and…

Pow. Magic, pure and simple.

"Hello," he said.

"Hi." She got out the word with a breathy sigh.

Since the kids were all upstairs, she figured it was safe to drag him into the foyer, shut the door and pretty much hurl herself into his waiting arms.

He laughed, the sound so rich and deep and warm, as he cradled her close. "Glad to see me, huh?"

"Ecstatic. Euphoric. Overjoyed. In seventh heaven…"

He put a finger to her lips. "A little less talk," he whispered. "And a lot more kissing."

Sounded like a fine idea to her. She lifted her mouth to him and the kissing commenced—a long, slow, lovely one. When they came up for air, she only pulled his head down again for another kiss that was every bit as pulse-pounding and toe-curling as the first one.

"Better watch it," he advised as he lifted his head for a second time. "We don't want to get too crazy—I mean, with the kids in the house."

"You are so right. Just one more…"

"Don't tempt me."

"You know you love it."

He grinned then. "You're right. I do."

She was just pulling his head down to steal a third kiss when a bloodcurdling scream erupted from upstairs.

Chapter Twelve

"My God. That sounds like Michael…." Megan whirled and raced for the stairs. She took them two at a time, Greg right behind her.

Olivia was waiting at the top, white as a sheet, eyes enormous with fright. "Aunt Megan, Michael's bleeding…."

Michael wailed again. And Anthony came running up the stairs. "What's going on? Is somebody screaming?"

Megan blinked. "I thought you were in your room with Michael."

"Uh. No…"

Michael screamed again. Megan took off along the upper hall as fast as her suddenly shaky legs would carry her. The door to the room the boys shared stood wide open.

"Michael? Michael, are you…?" Megan stopped in the doorway, words deserting her.

Michael sat on his bed, rocking, gripping his left hand with his right. Blood poured from between his fingers. There was blood on his cargo shorts, blood on his T-shirt, blood staining the blue bedspread patterned with a tumble of footballs, baseballs and soccer balls. His little face was pinched, dead-white with pure terror. "Aunt Megan, Aunt Megan, I cut my finger off!"

"Oh, honey." She rushed to him. Greg and the kids piled into the doorway. "A towel," she commanded. "Hurry…."

Greg was back in an instant with one of Angela's pretty green bathroom towels. Megan wrapped it around Michael's index finger, scooped him up and carried him to the bathroom.

He continued to wail as she rinsed the wound in the sink. At least, with some of the blood washed away, she could see the extent of the problem: not the whole finger, thank God. Only the top section, from the base of the nail up.

She got the big first aid kit from under the sink and wrapped his finger in gauze, took a clean towel and wrapped that around the gauze. Then she scooped him up into her arms again. "See if you can keep it raised up high, honey, until we get you to the doctor…."

Michael was beyond keeping anything high. He clutched his injured hand to his chest and went on sobbing.

Greg, who stood in the doorway, Olivia and Anthony on either side of him, had his cell phone to his ear. "I've got 911. They say they can reattach it. If we can find it."

Michael wailed again and pulled away from Megan's embrace just enough to point with his good hand. "Little table…by my bed…" He burst into a fresh flood of frantic tears and collapsed against Megan once more.

Greg left the doorway. Within seconds, he returned, the phone still at his ear. "All right," he said into it, "will do." He flipped it shut and stuck it in a pocket. "It's there—I think," he told Megan.

"You *think?*"

"It's so small—and there's blood all over it. It's next to an open pocketknife."

Pocketknife?

Michael didn't have a pocketknife…but Anthony did. "Oh, God. Anthony." She sent her other nephew a furious scowl.

He shook his head. "Uh-uh. My knife is locked up in the case like always. It's prob'ly the one that Dad gave him."

"Your father gave Michael a *pocketknife?*" It was the first Megan had heard of such a thing—and she would bet Angela didn't know about it, either.

Now, Anthony was bobbing his head. "Every time we'd go with Dad, Michael kept asking him for one like mine. So finally, he got him one. Dad told him to put it away safe until he was older and—"

"Hey." Greg interrupted, as Michael let out

another agonized wail. "Can we worry about the knife later?"

Megan gulped and nodded.

Greg added, "Right now, we need something to carry it in—a plastic bag, they told me. A plastic bag in another container with crushed ice and water."

Megan turned to Olivia. "Honey, run downstairs and show Greg where the zip bags and plastic containers are."

Olivia only stared—until Greg took her gently by the shoulders and knelt so they were eye to eye. "Olivia. Can you show me? Show me real quick?"

"Yes," the little girl whispered. Greg let her go and she ran for the stairs. He followed.

"It hurts, it hurts, it hurts…." Michael sobbed and moaned. Megan lowered herself carefully to the edge of the tub and rocked him, promising him over and over that it would be all right. Anthony, solemn and wide-eyed, dared to enter the bathroom with them. He came close and patted Michael's shaking shoulder.

An endless couple of minutes later, Greg and Olivia reappeared with a plastic bowl half-filled with crushed ice and water, a lid, and a sandwich-size Baggie.

"We need gauze," Greg said, "to wrap it in…."

Megan tipped her head toward the first-aid kit she'd left open on the counter. He took a couple of squares of gauze from it, went to the boys' bedroom and came back with the bit of finger, which he rinsed at the sink, wrapped in clean gauze and put in the Baggie. Olivia held out the plastic container. Greg took it, put the Baggie in it and snapped on the lid.

By then, Michael was chanting between sobs, "It hurts, it hurts, oh, it really hurts...."

Greg asked, "Want me to carry him down?"

"No. I can do it."

"All right, then. I'll drive." He turned to the other kids, who stared, white-faced. "Come on, you two." He gestured with the covered plastic bowl. "We're all going to the hospital."

Olivia nodded. Anthony gulped. Obedient as lambs, they turned to trail after Greg as he headed for the stairs.

Megan stroked Michael's clammy hair. "Honey, keep that towel around your finger. We're going to take you to the hospital now."

"It hurts, it hurts. Aunt Megan, it hurts...."

"I know. The doctor will make it all better real soon." She gathered him closer. Easing one hand under his legs and putting the other at his back, she stood. He clung to her, cowering close, sobbing and moaning.

"All better," she promised. "Good as new, you'll see...."

Greg had brought his own car, a sporty, silver BMW. Olivia and Anthony scrambled over the seat to the back, leaving the passenger door wide for Megan and Michael.

It was all such a frantic, mad, scary rush that Megan didn't even notice Carly until she and Michael reached the car. Carly stood out in her front yard in a pink visor and gardening gloves, staring.

Even from three houses down, Megan could see the stark misery on her pretty face.

Megan looked away. Right then, there was no time to worry about how Carly Alderson was taking seeing Greg drive off with Megan and a carful of kids. She tried to get Michael to sit in the back seat, where he would be safest and have his own seat belt, but he clung to her and cried even harder. She gave in and let him sit in her lap, hooking the seat belt over both of them.

Greg passed Anthony the covered plastic bowl. "Take good care of this."

"I will," he vowed.

Greg gunned the powerful engine and they were out of there. As soon as they turned the corner, he handed Megan his cell phone. "Call your sister. They have to have her permission to treat Michael—and she needs to know what's going on, anyway."

Megan had her sister's work number memorized. Luckily, she caught Angela at her desk. As calmly as she could, with Michael crying in her ear, she told her what was happening.

Angela wasted no time on freaking out. She got right to what needed doing. "I'll call Emergency at Rosewood Regional and tell them you're coming and that I'm on my way."

Megan asked, "Do you want to talk to—"

Angela cut her off. "Bad idea. He'll only cry harder. Just tell him I'll be there to meet him at the hospital…."

* * *

At Emergency, Greg drove up under the circular porte cochere entrance and let Megan and Michael off. "I'll park and be in with the other kids in a minute." He glanced over the seat. "Anthony?"

"Here." The boy passed the plastic bowl to Greg, who got out, went around and held the car door for Megan. He handed her the container as she turned for the entrance.

Inside, the clerk at the entry desk was ready for them. "Michael Buffington, right? This little boy's mother already called."

Michael only let out another pitiful sob and buried his head against Megan's shoulder. The clerk, unruffled, asked the pertinent questions and filled in the form for Megan, as Michael clutched his injured hand to his little chest and cried.

Angela came in with Greg and the kids.

"Mama!" Michael cried at the sight of her. "Mama! My finger…" Angela stepped up and Megan handed him over. A fresh flood of tears coursed down Michael's plump cheeks. "Mommy, I hurt. I hurt so bad…."

"I know you do, sweetheart. I know you do…." Angela rocked him, kissed his flushed little face and made more comforting noises as the inside doors swung open and a nurse came through with an empty wheelchair. Angela tried to settle Michael in the chair.

But he clutched her with his good hand and wailed in frantic pain and misery, "No, no. Mama, Mama…"

"I'll just carry him," she said.

The nurse frowned. "It's procedure. He should be in the chair."

"Forget procedure," Greg said darkly. "The boy wants his mother and it won't hurt a thing if she carries him in."

The nurse gave up. She took the plastic container from Megan and set it on the empty chair. "All right, then. Let's go." She wheeled the chair through the doors. Angela, carrying the sobbing Michael, went through at her side.

With a low, hydraulic hiss, the doors swung shut behind them.

An hour later, Michael, calm now, but still looking small and lost in the grown-up wheelchair, emerged from behind the wide doors, his mom at his side. His little hand was encased in a thick, snowy mitt of white gauze. His eyes drooped from pain medication.

The doctor came out a moment later to give Angela a few more instructions. Since the boy was so young, he said, recovery should be quick. The finger was likely to heal without scarring or loss of sensation.

"He'll be good as new in a month or two," the doctor promised. They were letting him go home for the night, but Angela should bring him in the next day, just to make sure that everything was okay.

Since they had two cars, Megan drove Michael and Angela in Angela's car. Greg took Anthony and Olivia in the BMW. Now that Michael was calm,

Angela put him in back, safely strapped in, and took the seat beside him.

By the time they got home, Michael was dead to the world. He didn't stir as Angela unhooked him from the seat belt and gathered him into her arms.

Inside, Megan hurried up the stairs ahead of mother and son, leading the way to the boys' room, where she rushed to strip off the bloody bedspread, wipe up the blood on the bed table and remove the offending pocketknife.

Angela saw the knife. She whispered, "Is that how he cut himself?"

Megan nodded. "I'll tell you all about it. Later..." Leaving Angela to put her injured little boy to bed, she carried the spread down to the laundry room and put it in the washer. Once she had the machine going, she went out to the kitchen, rinsed and dried the knife, folded it up and put it in a cabinet—high up, in the back—where it would be safe from small hands.

She turned to find Greg standing in the door from the dining room, watching her. "Oh!" She squeaked in surprise and put her hand to her chest.

"Sorry." The warmth in his eyes said he wasn't *that* sorry. "Didn't mean to scare you. Just admiring the view." He reported, "Anthony's in the living room hooked up to his Game Boy. And Olivia went upstairs, I think."

Megan realized she'd yet to thank him for what a huge help he'd been. "You've been wonderful about all this."

"It was no hardship, honestly. Men like to feel… useful."

"Well, you were. Definitely—more than useful. Indispensable."

He covered the distance between them and rested his hands to either side of her on the counter, trapping her in the middle. "Show me your gratitude."

"Love to." She kissed him, a chaste kiss, in consideration of the fact that they were in her sister's kitchen and likely to be interrupted at any time. "More later," she whispered, when he lifted his head.

"Can't wait—and what else can we do to help out around here?"

As it turned out, there was still Michael's pain medication and antibiotics to pick up. Megan volunteered to run over to Wal-Mart, where the pharmacy would still be open. Greg insisted on driving her.

It took awhile for the pharmacist to fill the prescriptions. To pass the time, they wandered around the big store. As they strolled up and down the wide aisles, Megan found herself thinking of the way Irene had snubbed her at Rosewood Market, of the crushed look on Carly's face when she'd seen Megan getting into Greg's car….

Lots of people went to Wal-Mart. The chances of running into a mutual acquaintance were pretty good here. Megan dreaded that someone else from the neighborhood would see them together and judge them—and spread more rumors about them.

Greg must have picked up on her growing anxiety. In the home electronics section, as they browsed the racks of CDs, he asked her if something was bothering her.

It really didn't seem like the time or the place to talk about it, so she sent him a bright smile—and told a white lie. "No. Nothing. Just, you know, a little stressed out after all the excitement."

He caught her arm in a gentle grip and turned her to face him. "Michael will be fine. If there was something to worry about, they'd have kept him at the hospital."

She nodded—and eased away from his touch. "I know. Yes."

He frowned at her reaction. But he let it go. They headed back to the pharmacy area, picked up the medications and returned to the house, where they found Angela in the kitchen whipping up some pasta with meat sauce to feed her hungry crew.

She turned from the stove with a wide smile for both of them as Megan set the prescriptions on the island counter. "Terrific. And Greg—I can't thank you enough. I'm so sorry that your first time here to see Megan had you heading straight for the hospital."

Greg laughed. "I didn't mind. I was glad to help."

Megan beamed up at him. "He actually had sense enough to call 911 and get some instructions."

He shrugged the compliments away. "No big deal. Honestly."

"Well, thank you again…." Angela tasted the

sauce and set the spoon in the spoon rest. "And I know you two didn't plan to stick around here forever. As of now, you are both officially dismissed. Take off and have a great evening—what's left of it, anyway."

Megan still needed to talk to Angela about Jerome giving Michael that pocketknife, but she supposed she would have to wait for a more appropriate time. Greg had been incredible about everything. She couldn't ask him to wait even longer while she and Angela got into it about the problems with Jerome— which Angela really wouldn't feel comfortable discussing with Greg around, anyway.

She wondered if Angela would try to call Jerome and let him know what had happened. Angela always did her best to play fair with the kids' father, to keep him informed of their troubles and triumphs.

Really, Ange did need to know about the knife before she called him....

Greg said good-night to Angela and headed for the foyer. Still thinking about that pocketknife, Megan followed him out.

He stopped at the door and turned to her. "How about tomorrow night? Could you swing it, do you think?"

"Hey," she teased. "Wait a minute. Tonight's not over yet."

"Yeah, it is."

She started to protest—and then she realized: he *got* it. He understood that things still needed dealing with here at home. "Oh, Greg…"

He said, "I know you and your sister have to handle the pocketknife issue. And besides, I think she'd really appreciate it about now if you stuck around."

"You're sure? You don't mind?"

"Not as long as I can see you tomorrow. Same time?"

She had way too much work to do to take two evenings off in a row. But she would manage it somehow. "Tomorrow," she promised, and then remembered her plan to go to him in Manhattan, to avoid being seen with him in town. "How about this? When Angela gets home, I'll take the train down to the city and meet you at—"

He was shaking his head. "Uh-uh. It would be nearly eight by the time you got there. I'm coming here. At four-thirty. Same as today—only tomorrow I'm hoping we'll get lucky and avoid the thrills and chills of a visit to the E.R."

She really did need to have a long talk with him about keeping things a little more…low-key. Very soon. Like tomorrow…. "Okay, then." She put on a bright smile. "Four-thirty."

He tipped her chin up with a finger. "Is there a problem? You seem a little…I don't know. Doubtful, maybe. Unsure…."

They could talk about it tomorrow. She evaded the actual question, sliding her hands up around his neck, lifting on tiptoe. "I'm fine."

"Good." He brushed a soft kiss across her mouth, making her lips tingle and sending a wash of warmth cascading through her.

* * *

When she walked back into the kitchen, Angela blinked. "Forget something?"

Megan went to the sink, flipped on the faucet and squirted soap on her hands. "Green salad?"

"Huh?"

She rinsed her hands and reached for the towel. "Greg's gone. He'll be back tomorrow, but tonight he said he thought I'd want to stick around here—which I do."

Angela started protesting. "Oh, that's silly. You don't need to—"

"Yes, I do need to. Now, quit arguing and answer my question."

"What question?"

"Green salad?"

"You're sure?"

"Positive—and it's okay. Truly. He'll be here tomorrow. It'll all work out fine."

Since Michael was still sleeping, they sat down to eat without him. Angela frowned at Anthony and asked how Michael had gotten his hands on his big brother's pocketknife.

Anthony cried, "But it wasn't my knife!"

Once she'd heard the real story, Angela said quietly, "Your father shouldn't have given Michael a knife. I'll have to talk to him about it."

Instantly, Anthony jumped to Jerome's defense. "But Michael kept *bugging* him about it. What could Dad do?"

"Say no—but that's not your concern. I'll discuss it with your father later."

"But Dad was only trying to—"

"Anthony. That's enough. Eat your spaghetti."

After the meal, there were baths and bedtime stories. Finally, the two older kids went to bed—and then Michael woke up, crying; the medication they'd given him at the hospital had worn off.

Angela gave him his medicine, convinced him to slurp up a little chicken noodle soup, and then sat with him in the big chair in the living room until he dropped off. When those blue eyes finally drooped shut, she carried him back upstairs and tucked him into bed again.

Downstairs once more, she called Jerome. She used the kitchen extension. Megan went on into the living room so her sister could have the privacy to say what needed saying.

It was only five minutes or so before Angela was dropping down next to her on the sofa.

Megan asked gingerly, "How did it go?"

Angela cast a glance toward the ceiling. "Jerome is Jerome and his own bad judgment is somehow never his fault."

"Sorry, sis."

"Yeah. Me, too…" Angela sank onto the cushions and lazily turned her head Megan's way. "On a happier note, I'm glad at least one of us has good taste in men."

Megan flopped back and sank down until she was eye to eye with her sister. "Greg was wonderful today, wasn't he?"

Ange agreed. "Absolutely the best. It's so funny. When he lived in the neighborhood, we hardly ever saw him. He was always working, rarely at home. And he was nice enough, but distant, didn't you think? He always seemed...preoccupied, then. He comes across as so much more relaxed now. A happier man, you know?"

"Umm..." Megan's dreamy grin faded a little as she remembered Irene at the market. And Carly, so pretty and so very sad, standing in front of her huge, empty McMansion in her gardening gloves and sun visor.

"Okay," said Angela. "Why the long face?"

"My reputation is in shreds."

Angela chuckled. "Lucky for you this is the twenty-first century. Nowadays, people do what they want to do, and they don't waste a lot of time worrying about what the neighbors are going to say."

"Too bad that here in Rosewood, the neighbors are still gossiping just as much as they ever did back in the bad old days." Megan pretended to shiver. "I mean, can you believe it? *I'm* the 'other woman.' That is so not me. I'm everybody's best friend—the woman everybody else can talk to. I'm no threat. If you'd asked me a month ago, I would have sworn to you that I would never get myself in a position like this. I am not and never have been the husband-stealing type."

Angela chided, "How many times do I have to remind you that Greg and Carly are divorced—not to mention that you're way too concerned about what other people think?"

"I think I sense a lecture coming on."

Angela widened her blue eyes. "Me? Lecture you? Never."

Megan blew out a breath. "Okay. Yeah. I know I worry too much about other people talking. But, well, they *are* talking. And it *does* bother me."

"You're sure they're talking—that it's not just you *thinking* that they are?"

Megan told her about Irene, in the market that day. And about Rhonda's little visit on Saturday.

Angela advised, "Ignore them. Those two aren't worth the time it takes to get upset at them."

"I know you're right. But it just seems like, well, this thing between Greg and me…it's happening so fast."

Angela reached across and lightly squeezed her arm. "*Too* fast, you mean?"

"I'm totally gone on him—but yeah. Maybe. Too fast."

"Talk to him. Tell him you need to…slow down a little."

"I will. Tomorrow. He's coming at four-thirty. He'll hang out with me and the kids until you get home, and then I think he's taking me out to dinner or something."

"He does like kids, I noticed."

"Yeah. He does."

"Still, he and Carly never had any…"

"Greg told me that at first, he wanted to and she wasn't ready. Then, by the end, *she* wanted to—and he felt they just had too many problems to solve."

"Sad, huh? The way things work out some-times…." The faraway look in Angela's eyes had

Megan wondering who she was really talking about—Greg and Carly or her own failed marriage? Then her sister smiled. "Did I mention that I do think Greg's a terrific guy?"

"Yes, Ange. You did."

"And I'm taking a family day tomorrow to look after Michael, so you're off the hook as far as the kids go."

That news had Megan popping up straight on the couch. "I could meet him in the city, after all."

"Well, yeah. I guess you could."

She jumped to her feet. "I'm calling him right now."

"No way," said Greg. "It has to be Rosewood."

"Er, it does?"

"That's right."

"Why?"

"You'll find out. Tomorrow." He seemed really pleased with himself, so pleased that she didn't have the heart to ruin whatever it was he had planned. "I miss you. Already," he said.

And she clutched the phone tighter and said, "I miss you, too," and realized she meant it with all of her heart.

"Dress casual," he instructed. "Flat shoes."

"Well, all right…"

"Four-thirty," he said. "Be ready."

"Yes, Master."

"I do like the way you say that." She could tell he was smiling. And then he whispered, "Good night, Megan," and he was gone.

* * *

All the next day, while she plowed through the mountain of work in front of her, Megan practiced how she'd tell him that she needed to take things a little slower, that she didn't want to meet him in Rosewood anymore, not for a while, anyway. That she would come down to the city whenever she could get away—and that she did, after all, have to go to Banning's, Inc. every couple of weeks, at least, now they had a contract to fulfill. So of course, they could be together for the evening then….

By the time he drove up at four-thirty, she knew just what she would say.

But when she opened the front door and saw him standing there on the step in faded jeans and a T-shirt, wearing that crooked smile that stopped her heart, a stack of cartoon DVDs cradled in those big, strong arms…

Suddenly, all those carefully planned speeches deserted her. She didn't want to talk about what would happen from here on out. She just wanted to be with him.

She wanted to spend the afternoon and the evening at his side. In Rosewood, out of Rosewood. In Manhattan.

On the moon. In Timbuktu….

She wanted today. And any day they could get together. Somehow, she would learn to take her sister's advice and ignore the people who didn't deserve her attention in the first place.

And as for poor Carly, well, slowly, her hurt would heal. She'd get over Greg, stop waiting for him to come back to her. Until she did get over him, she was going to be suffering—whether she saw Greg with someone else or not.

And besides, at least half the time, Megan would be going to *him*. If they got lucky, they might see each other for months and never again run into anyone from the neighborhood.

He glanced down at the DVDs in his arms. "I thought Michael might be getting stir-crazy about now. Maybe a few movies will help...."

"A few? You've got at least twenty there."

His smile was rueful. "I had no clue which ones he might already have."

They took the DVDs upstairs, where Michael, already bored with being an invalid, brightened considerably at the sight of all those movies.

"Oh, wow," he said. "Cool. *Aladdin! Shrek 2! A Shark's Tale!*" He picked up each DVD in turn and exclaimed over it.

Angela thanked Greg for his thoughtfulness and, with a definite twinkle in her eye, told them to have a great time.

When they went out the front door, Megan didn't so much as glance toward Carly's house. If Carly was out there on her broad, green slope of front law, looking dejected, so be it. It wasn't Megan's fault that Carly's marriage was over.

Greg held the passenger door for her and Megan settled into the leather seat. When he slid in behind the wheel, she asked, "All right. So where are we going?"

"You'll see."

"You are just so mysterious."

"Won't be long now...."

Five blocks later, he was pulling into the driveway of his house. The garage door trundled up and he drove in.

"Hmm. Another visit to your empty house," she said. "Is there something I missed the first time?"

He gave her a smug grin. "Not so empty now."

She looked down at her T-shirt and jeans. "Flat shoes and casual clothes, you said." She sent him a knowing look. "Your furniture arrived—and we're going to be unpacking everything and arranging the pieces."

"That's right. Some date, huh?"

"The best. I not only got to pick out most of your furniture, I also get to tell you where to put it."

"That's my plan."

"Do I get takeout?"

"Pizza, Chinese—you name it."

"Chinese. Later." She rubbed her hands together. "But right now, let's get started."

"Wait." He caught one hand and pressed a kiss on the tip of the longest finger. "There's an extra surprise—beyond how hard you get to work for your egg roll and pot stickers."

She laughed. "What more could there possibly be?"

He paused for effect before proudly announcing,

"I've decided I'm through living in the city. I want us to have more time together, to take this thing between us…wherever it goes. So I'm moving back to Rosewood. ASAP."

Chapter Thirteen

There it was, Greg thought. That strange look in her eyes again....

The look he'd seen more than once yesterday. The faraway look, the one that told him there was something going on with her.

Something...not good.

Twice yesterday, he'd asked her what was wrong. She'd claimed there was nothing. And both times, just like now, her green gaze had slid away....

He should ask her again, and he knew it. Say, *What's the matter, Megan? Stop evading. Tell me. What's wrong?*

But damned if he wasn't afraid of her answer.

And the fact that he feared what she might tell him....

That bugged the hell out of him. It more than bugged him. It made his gut churn and his heart pound out a rhythm of heavy, sick dread. It had him thinking that there could be a downside to going crazy over a woman. After all, the crazier a man got for a woman, the more she might hurt him.

There had been a time when Carly could hurt him—and she had. Deeply. By turning away from him in all the ways that really mattered, by keeping her heart a secret from him, by making their lives a dry, bloodless exercise in going through the motions.

That had been bad.

This, though—what he felt for Megan...

It was stronger, deeper, hotter—right from the first. With Carly, looking back now, he could see that there'd always been a certain distance between them. She'd looked up to him, deferred to him, put herself second to him. At the time, that had seemed like the way it *should* be.

But now he knew better. Now he wanted a true equal, a woman to stand beside him.

And Megan was that—more than that. So much more.

Megan had it all: a big heart and a great sense of humor; that round, ripe, so-sexy body, and a brilliant head for business. She got to him in some undeniable, basic way. She had from that first moment he'd really seen her, in his office, on the eve of Independence Day.

From that very first moment she'd walked in the

door, he couldn't even look at her without wanting to grab her and hold her—and never, ever let her go.

Seventeen days, since that first day. Hardly more than a couple of weeks. And yet, somehow, in that short space of time, it was getting so it wasn't only about how much he wanted her, how much he wanted to *be* with her. It was getting so he couldn't imagine his life without her in it. As if, without her, some vital part of himself would die.

That was damn scary.

That was the thing that, for the first time, had Greg Banning thinking that maybe his cold, distant, untouchable parents had the right idea, after all. If you didn't let yourself care too much, you couldn't get hurt too much, could you?

"Oh, Greg," Megan whispered.

What the hell did that mean? Oh, Greg, I'm nuts for you? Oh, Greg, I'm not sure about you and me?

Oh, Greg, kiss me…?

He decided he wouldn't ask. He'd go for the kiss.

And he did, reaching across the console, taking her flushed face in his hands, leaning close to breathe in the faint, arousing scent of flowers and peaches that always seemed to cling to her skin.

"Megan…" His voice came out low and rough with desire and confusion. He took her mouth, hard, so she gasped a little—and then, almost instantly, he felt her soften, opening to him, swaying closer, a low moan escaping her. He drank in the surrendering sound, tasting her more deeply, running his tongue over the slick, hot surfaces beyond her parted lips.

With another moan, she swayed even closer, giving herself up completely to his kiss. He took what she offered, threading the fingers of one hand up into the silky fall of her hair, cupping her head more firmly—and freeing his other hand to touch her.

And he did touch her. He ran a slow finger down the side of her neck, tracing the V-shaped collar of her T-shirt.

Her breasts were so round and full. So beautiful…

He took one in his hand, flicking at the nipple through her shirt and bra, feeling the hard, needful little nub even through her clothes. She shivered, gasped again. He drank in the sound.

His own arousal strained at his jeans. He *always* wanted her, but now, at this minute, the longing was a pulse that beat through his veins, demanding…now! Now, now…

He broke the kiss. She moaned in protest and surged up, trying to recapture his lips. Fingers tangled in her hair, he held her still, his mouth an inch from hers. "Inside the house," he growled. "Now…"

Her eyelids were low. She sighed. "Yes. Oh, yes…"

They couldn't get out of that car fast enough. Her side was closest to the inner door. She got there ahead of him and waited, her eyes the green of a secret pool, her body swaying toward him as if magnetized.

"Oh, Greg…" This time he had no doubt what the words meant: she wanted him.

As he wanted her….

She reached out with a tiny cry. He caught her in his arms, wrapped her tight against him, kissed her again. Because she wanted it. Because he couldn't resist.

He pushed her back to the door, and ground his hips against her. It was agony, the sweetest kind of torture, the kind that turns a man inside out, that makes him forget the shadows in a woman's eyes.

Her little shirt ended right above the low waist of her jeans. He dipped his hands up under it, felt the full, sweet, giving flesh of her midsection, ran his palms up her rib cage, over her bra—and around to the back.

A flick of his thumb and index finger and the clasp let go. He pushed the bra out of his way, easing his hands beneath it, so he could cup those beautiful, soft breasts. She sighed into his mouth, her nipples, hard with yearning, poking into the center of his palms.

She touched him—and it nearly finished him— her soft, stroking hand finding its way down between their tight-pressed bodies. She cupped him through his jeans, her hand curling around him lengthwise, covering him, rubbing him.

He thought he would die—and not mind at all. Go out in a blaze of mindless, lust-bright glory.

She was a woman with a mission and she went to work, kissing him madly, rubbing her round, hot body against him, all the while stroking him, unhooking the metal buttons at the front of his jeans, one and then the other, slipping his boxers out of the way.

Until she had him, naked, in her hand.

He let out a moan dragged up from the depths of him. And she wrapped her fingers snug around him, brushing a naughty thumb over the nerve-thick head, catching the bit of moisture that wept from him, spreading it around....

She laughed, a low, rough sound of pleasure, of excitement. "Now," she pleaded—a plea that was somehow, at the same time, a bold command. "Now, Greg. Please..."

He had a condom—more than one. He'd thought that after dinner and a glass of wine, at the end of the evening, they might try out his new bed.

So much for waiting to use the bed....

He reached behind him, fumbled in a pocket of the jeans she'd pushed halfway down his hips. He pulled one out and then brought it between them.

With a pleased little purring sound, she took it, peeled the wrapper off with eager hands and rolled it down over him. He moaned as she did that; he whispered her name. "Megan..."

"Yes," she breathed with another low, sexy laugh, as her flat canvas shoes went flying. "Oh, yes...." She unbuttoned the snap at the waist of her jeans. She brought the zipper down. The small, rasping sound as the teeth parted drove him crazy. Insane. Stark, raving out of his mind.

To have her. Now. To be inside her, right here, standing up, against the door....

She skimmed the jeans off and away, her sexy, lacy panties with them. He took her by the hips, lifting her. She wrapped those full thighs around him.

He entered her in a slow, even glide. Her body opened like a liquid flower for him, giving him no resistance. Only wetness, heat and welcome. She took him in—deep. All the way. They both threw back their heads and moaned at the sheer aching pleasure of it.

And after that, it was quick and wild, fierce and mindless....

He braced her against the door and she locked those fine, big legs around him as she rode him, hard, rolling her hips against him, crying out in excitement, meeting his every thrust with one of her own.

He held her, with the help of the door. And the world burst wide open—open so far that it seemed to turn itself inside out. He felt her coming....

That did it. He went over, too, pressing himself hard up into her, holding her hips to keep her in place. With a low groan, he sagged against the door, waves of pleasure tingling along every nerve. Smelling of peaches and musk, her skin moist from loving, she rained soft kisses on his lips, his chin, his jaw, his neck....

Finally, she unclasped her ankles from their tight grip around him. Gently, with great care, he lowered her to the step. She clung to his neck, burying her head in his shoulder.

He kissed her hair and whispered, still half-breathless, "So much for a nice bottle of wine and fresh sheets on my new bed."

She giggled and nipped his ear. "We could still do the wine. And the bed. Eventually."

"Then we'd damn well better get busy."

"You are so right. Button up, big boy. Let's get to work."

They did make it to his new bed. Well after midnight.

By then, every room had furniture in it, attractively arranged. Also, most of the kitchen stuff and linens had been put away. He still had more work to do, to get everything where it belonged.

But it was livable. He could move in.

And he planned to. On Saturday. Once he was in, little by little he would be moving stuff from the apartment to Rosewood. And in a few weeks, he would be selling off whatever goods and furniture he couldn't use, putting his place in the city up for sale.

They didn't talk about any of that, though—about when he would move in, about his plans for the Manhattan apartment and its contents. Greg wasn't sure which of them was avoiding the subject. He decided it didn't matter.

He'd told her he was coming back to live in Rosewood; he'd hit the main point. If she wanted to know more about his plans, she could ask.

In his new bed, late that night, he took care to make the loving slow and lazy, to make it last. He looked down at her flushed face beneath him as he moved in long, slow strokes within her, and he thought that he'd never seen a woman so soft and open to loving, a woman so right for him....

Strangely, in the passion and the wonder of it, there was sadness for him, too. And an edge that might have been the beginnings of anger....

He pushed those darker emotions away. He denied them. He concentrated on the woman in his arms, on giving her pleasure, on taking it back in kind.

Afterward, she smiled so sweetly up at him. She whispered with a yawn that she really did have to get going. He watched her eyes drift shut.

She sighed. "I think I'll just lie here with you, for a minute or two...."

He watched her fall asleep. And he didn't wake her. She was only a few blocks from home and could get over there in a flash come morning. A lock of her wavy blond hair had fallen across her cheek. With a finger, he guided it away, smoothing it on the pillow. Then he pulled up the sheet and gathered her close.

It took him a long while to fall asleep.

Megan woke to daylight. She blinked at the slits of sunlight peeking through the cherry-wood blinds—and sat bolt upright with a cry.

Beside her, Greg grumbled, "Huh?" Yawning

hugely, he dragged himself to a sitting position. "What's up?"

"I'm late." She picked up the alarm from the nightstand and shook it at him. "Greg. It's 8:00 a.m."

He squinted at it. "Yep. Sure is." And he yawned again. "Looks like I'm going to be late for work, too. But it's no big deal. Not this once. I've got no major meetings or anything…."

"Good to hear," she muttered dryly, as she threw back the sheet and scrambled for her scattered clothes. He just sat there, looking sexy and sleepy, his hair sticking up every which way, all manly muscles and a come-back-here-and-kiss-me-baby smile. She shook out her panties with a hard snap and shoved her legs into them. "Come on. Get dressed." She grabbed his jeans from the pile of clothes on the floor and threw them at him. He caught them, still grinning. She scowled. "In case you didn't notice, I desperately need a ride home— right now."

He pretended to sulk. "I was going to make lattes."

"You don't have any coffee." She got her jeans, stuck her legs into them, yanked them up and buttoned them.

"I could buy some—and did you know you have the cutest butt of any woman around? So full and tempting. A shame to cover it up…."

"Sorry, no time to buy coffee. I have to get to work."

"You work too hard. You should take a day off."

"Can't. But about my butt…"

"Umm?" He laced his hands behind his head, causing the muscles in his big arms to bunch in the most amazing way. She stared. She couldn't help herself. He prompted, looking smug, "You were saying, about your butt?"

"So glad you like it."

"I do."

"Get dressed." She threw his boxers at him, grabbed her bra, which was all tangled up, and set about straightening it out so she could put it on.

At last, grumbling, "You're no fun," he threw back the covers and strutted toward the bath, looking like something that had walked right off the page of a really fine beefcake calendar: Mr. July, in the flesh.

She tried not to watch him walk away. It was very difficult, not watching him. And not drooling? That was kind of hard, too. Once he'd shut the bathroom door, she sucked in a big breath, let it out slowly and put on her bra.

Marti Vincente, trim and pulled-together as always in black capris and a white cap-sleeved shirt, was out watering her hydrangeas when Greg pulled into the driveway. Megan waved. Marti paused just a fraction of a second before waving back—and she wasn't smiling.

Greg got out of the car and went with Megan to the breezeway door. Every step of the way, she was aware of Marti next door, watering the flowers, barely pausing to wave.

What was Marti thinking?

Megan shut her eyes and told herself she wouldn't dwell on it. Greg was going to be living in Rosewood soon. They *would* be running into the neighbors. More often than she had previously anticipated.

She needed to get used to the funny looks and the watchful expressions. For a while, that was probably just how it was going to be.

Greg waited for her to unlock the breezeway door and then went inside with her. Once safely out of sight of the street, she turned to him. He tipped up her chin and brushed a kiss on her mouth, and she thought how he was the greatest guy in the whole wide world.

The greatest guy, truly....

She'd never met a man like him. So kind and funny and patient and good.

Not to mention a pure pleasure to look at. And magic in bed.

"Thanks," she said, meaning it. "I had a terrific time...."

His fine mouth quirked up at one corner. "Arranging my furniture for me, you mean?"

"That...and the Chinese. Love those pot stickers. And the wine was wonderful. The sex, too. That was..." She pretended to fan herself.

He kissed her once more. Quick and hard. And then, with a promise that he'd call her that evening, he went out the breezeway door, shutting it softly behind him.

Megan turned for the door to the backyard and the stairs up to her apartment. But after two steps, she paused, listening. She heard Greg's car start up and drive away.

And she wondered if Marti was still out there in her front yard. Why hadn't the older woman smiled at her? Why had she held back that extra second before raising her arm to wave?

Megan wondered…and felt about two inches tall. Marti was no Irene or Rhonda. She was a sweet woman with a smile for everyone—except, apparently, for Megan. Since Megan had moved into the neighborhood, she'd come to think of Marti as a friend.

It wasn't right. And Megan had to know—was Marti judging her, too?

She whirled, yanked the door open and marched through.

Marti was still out there, sprinkling the flowers. Megan went down the driveway, across the short section of sidewalk to Marti's driveway and up it. Marti, looking wary, watched her come.

"Marti?"

At last, her neighbor smiled—kind of a forced-looking one, but a smile nonetheless. "Megan. How have you been?"

"Better than ever. Mostly. But I do have…well, I wonder if we could talk. For a moment…."

"Certainly." Marti went and shut off the hose. She set it down on the grass. "Come inside. I've got some coffee on."

They sat at the breakfast table in Marti's amazing kitchen—a kitchen a lot like the one in Greg's new house. With top-of-the-line appliances, granite countertops and a big, curving island containing its own separate sink.

Marti served the coffee. Megan waited until she sat down before saying, "I noticed, just now, when Greg and I drove up, that you seemed a little hesitant to wave at me."

Marti stirred her coffee, though the cream she'd dribbled into it had already dissolved. "I…well, Megan, I really don't know what to say."

Megan's throat tightened. Her palms felt clammy. Somehow, though, when she spoke, her voice was clipped and firm. "Try the truth, okay? How about that?"

Marti looked miserable. "I'm sorry. I shouldn't judge you. But I am a good Catholic. I'm…old school, I guess you could say. I have never believed in divorce."

Megan coughed to clear her clutching throat. "You mean you don't approve of my going out with Greg because he's divorced?"

"Oh, no." Marti let out a nervous trill of laughter. "I'm not *that* old school. Life goes on. I understand. But Megan, what I can't accept is a woman who steals another woman's husband. That's adultery. And adultery is a sin."

With a sick, sinking feeling, Megan understood. "You think I went out with Greg *before,* don't you? When he lived in the neighborhood? When he was still married to Carly? Is that what you think?"

"Well, yes. That's what I heard. And from more than one source."

Chapter Fourteen

Something in Megan's expression must have gotten through to Marti. She set down her cup without drinking from it. "Oh, my Lord. It's not true, is it?"

Megan pressed her lips together and slowly shook her head. "Never," she vowed. "When Greg lived in the neighborhood, I never said more than two words to him, or he to me. We only got together a few weeks ago—*after* his divorce from Carly became final—when he hired me and my company to do some work for Banning's, Inc."

Marti pushed her cup away. "Oh, Megan. I'm ashamed, I truly am. I should have asked *you*...."

"Yes. You should have. And let me guess who told you that lie—Irene Dare. Rhonda Johnson. And probably a couple of other women who *know* Irene and Rhonda."

Marti cast a penitent glance heavenward. "Megan, forgive me. I should have known better than to listen to them. And I have no excuse for believing them. Except that, seeing you and Greg today, I jumped to the conclusion that since you're together now, you were probably getting together *then.*"

"It was the wrong conclusion."

"I see that now. And not that it helps any, but you can be sure that if anyone else tries to lay that line of baloney on me, I promise you, they'll get an earful. I'll tell them in no uncertain terms that they don't know what they're talking about."

Megan felt better—and worse—after talking to Marti.

Better, because Marti, who played hostess at the Vincente family restaurant, spoke with a lot of people on a daily basis. If anyone gossiped about Megan and Greg to Marti from now on, she would be setting them straight. That was good.

But the fact that the rumors about Megan and Greg had degenerated into outright lies of betrayal and adultery...

That made he feel worse. A lot worse.

And now Greg was moving back to town. There would be no escaping to the lovely anonymity of Manhattan. If she wanted to be with him, she'd be with him in Rosewood.

And people would talk.

* * *

Megan got to work an hour and a half late and went straight into a meeting that lasted till noon. She decided to skip lunch. She'd grab a protein bar at her desk and make a little headway on the horror show that was her workload.

But then she found Vanessa Banning waiting for her in one of the guest chairs outside her office. Greg's mother was dressed to kill in a fabulous lightweight silk suit of celadon-green, and impeccable Prada pumps—Megan knew they were Prada; she'd seen them in Saks' window just last Saturday.

Vanessa swept elegantly to her feet. "Megan. So good to see you…." She held out her fine-boned white hand.

Megan took it and gave it a quick shake. Cool as before. Did actual blood run in this woman's veins? "How are you, Vanessa?"

"Wonderful, wonderful."

"What can I do for you?"

"Well, I just thought it would be lovely if the two of us could steal an hour together, get to know each other a bit. I was thinking perhaps…lunch? Could you get away, do you think? I know it's sudden, but still, I *was* hoping…."

Greg's words from Sunday morning popped into Megan's mind: *You have to promise me never to let yourself be alone with her…*

Oh, really. He must have been exaggerating.

Megan asked, "Did you come all the way from Montauk?"

"As a matter of fact, no. I've stayed in Manhattan this past week. But I plan to return to the beach house. Very soon. As soon as I've dealt with what needs dealing with around here—and what do you say? Let me buy you lunch."

They went to a café Megan liked over on South. Unpretentious, with terrific food. A little pricey, but she figured Vanessa wouldn't mind paying for the best.

The meal started out just fine. Vanessa had a glass of white wine. Megan took iced tea; she had work to do when she got back to the office, a mountain of it, and she couldn't have her brain fogged by alcohol.

Vanessa had more questions about Megan's family. "So your adoptive parents divorced?"

"Yes."

"Do you ever see them?"

"My father remarried. We…don't really keep in touch."

"And your mother?"

"My mother lives in South Carolina now. She doesn't get back to Rosewood much."

"Ah. I see…."

More questions followed. Vanessa had a million of them. Megan answered honestly.

And then Vanessa mentioned Carly. Greg's mother took a tiny bite of her pan-seared salmon and delicately remarked how upset the "poor thing" was at the collapse of her marriage. Megan, slightly uncomfortable with the subject but willing to make the right noises, said that she really did like Carly and hoped, over time, that she and Carly might be friends again.

"Oh," said Vanessa, one perfectly waxed brow arching toward her hairline. "You and Carly are not only neighbors, but *friends?*" The cold light in her eye said she knew exactly the relationship Megan and Carly had shared—though how she would have found that out was a little beyond Megan. Not from Greg, Megan was sure.

"We *were* friends," she answered carefully.

"Until you…stole her husband, you mean?"

Megan set down her fork. Oh, goody. Defending herself against charges of adultery two times in one day. She had a sudden image of herself with a big red *A* painted on her forehead.

A for Adulteress.

How had this happened? All of a sudden she was living in an old-time novel, playing the part of the evil temptress, the heartless seducer of nice women's husbands. It was so not a role she'd ever imagined herself in.

Uh-uh. The pleasant hefty girl down the block, the one you could count on. That was more Megan's style.

She was getting a headache. And her stomach had suddenly clenched tight. "No, Vanessa, I did not steal Greg from Carly. They were already divorced when Greg and I started seeing each other." She placed her napkin at the side of her plate. "And I think maybe we—"

Vanessa didn't even let her get the whole sentence out. "Oh, now. Let's not get huffy. Put your napkin back in your lap and finish your lunch." She took a tiny sip of her pinot grigio. "Relax. Please." She smiled. A friendly smile.

Wasn't it?

More general talk followed. Megan began to enjoy the meal again and to think that it was all going along fine, after all. That moment about Carly…just a rough patch, soon forgotten.

But then, as Vanessa signaled for the check, it all went straight to hell. No detours. No chance to get out gracefully.

"I'm assuming you won't want dessert, now will you?" Vanessa asked. "You are really much too fat, you know." She clucked her tongue as Megan stared at her blankly in disbelief. "Yes." Vanessa sighed. "Too fat. With no background. An ambitious, dumpy little nobody from nowhere, USA."

Megan realized then that she should have gotten up and walked out back there at that first cruel remark regarding Carly. But no. She'd let herself be lulled by the absurd hope that she might somehow get to know and like Greg's mother.

She'd stayed till the bitter end. And now the seemingly pleasant little getting-to-know-you lunch had veered abruptly off into nightmareland.

Megan heard herself sputtering, "I…I don't—"

Vanessa cut her off with a bored wave of her bloodless hand. "Really. I'm sure you know perfectly well why I drove all the way up to Poughkeepsie today. I felt it was time for us to come to an understanding. I want you out of my son's life. He's a *Banning,* after all—in spite of that ridiculous, romantic egalitarian streak of his. He deserves so much better than some ordinary little *business*person like you. He needs to marry someone of his own circle—or go back to that pretty wife of his, for heaven's sake. At least she *tries,* the poor thing. She's not of our circle, but she does work hard to be the kind of wife Greg needs. Either. I can live with either, Carly, or someone more suitable. But not with *you.* Really. He must get rid of you."

Nightmareland. Oh, yeah. No doubt about it. Megan's head pounded and her stomach ached. She never should have agreed to have lunch with this woman; she should have listened to Greg.

And right now, all she wanted was out of there. She stood. Her napkin dropped to the floor. She left it there. "Greg told me not to be alone with you. Now I see why."

Vanessa gazed up at her, eyes like twin cubes of ice. "You will never by accepted by his family, or by anyone else who matters. Much wiser just to walk away now, don't you think?"

"Goodbye, Vanessa. Thank you for lunch." Megan hitched her tote on her shoulder and got out of there.

Chapter Fifteen

For the rest of the afternoon, Megan tried valiantly to keep her mind on her enormous workload and off the big problem of her relationship with Greg—and Greg's astonishingly awful mother. *And* the fact that Megan was now widely considered to be a cheap, low-down husband-stealer in her own hometown.

It just, well, it wasn't working out for her.

Her life was a big fat mess. She'd finally found a wonderful, sexy, thoughtful man with a great sense of humor who only wanted to be with her as she wanted to be with him....

And all she could think of was how she couldn't bear another date with him where someone from the neighborhood might see them and think all the wrong things about them. How, if she ever had to be in the same room with Vanessa Banning again, one of them would not come out alive.

At four, as always, she picked up the kids. Michael had been allowed—with a long list of special instructions—to go back to day camp that day.

The doorbell rang at five. The kids were all in the living room, watching one of the DVDs Greg had brought the day before.

What now? Megan thought as she went to the door. *Another neighbor looking for a chance to tell me what a slut I am? Or maybe just Vanessa, back for round two?*

Megan threw open the door, ready to do battle— and found Greg, still in his business clothes, a huge bouquet of flowers in his hand.

"I know, I was here yesterday. But for some reason, I just can't stay away."

She looked in his dear face and instantly wanted to grab him, hold on tight and burst into a flood of hurt, angry tears.

He must have picked up on her misery, because his expression darkened. "What's happened?"

She swallowed down the building emotion and ushered him over the threshold. Once he was safely inside with the door shut behind him, she confessed, "Bad day. Really, really bad day."

He set the flowers on the hall table and took her gently by the arms. "Tell me. Everything."

She blinked to make the stupid tears go away, and

gestured toward the living room where *The Incredibles* was playing. "The kids are here…."

He brushed a kiss across her mouth. In spite of her distress, the familiar thrill shimmered through her at the tender caress. He asked, "And Angela comes home…?"

Megan sniffed. "In forty-five minutes or so."

"Good. We can talk then."

"Yeah." She forced a brave smile, thinking that maybe she could get him to see how they needed to slow down a little. That she really couldn't take being the biggest man-stealer in Rosewood.

Biggest in the literal sense. Just ask his mother.

He was nodding as he reached for the flowers. "In the meantime, these could use a drink."

She took them from him. "They're gorgeous. Thank you…."

"My pleasure."

Megan put the flowers in a vase and they joined the kids in the living room for the last half of the movie. It was a great little film, but she had trouble concentrating on it. She kept going over how she would manage to explain to Greg that she was absolutely nuts for him—but, for a while, they needed to rethink spending so much time together.

Angela came home right on time. Megan got her vase of flowers and led Greg through the breezeway and up the back stairs to her apartment.

"This is nice," he said, surveying her Pottery Barn furniture and teal-blue walls hung with her own work. "Really nice." He looked so pleased, his expression so open and vulnerable. He sent her a warm smile. "Hard to believe this is the first time I've seen your place...."

She had one big living area, the kitchen divided off by a long jut of counter, her dining table on the living room side. She set the vase of flowers in the center of the table and gestured at the comfy buff-colored sectional sofa. "Beer or wine?"

"Doesn't matter." He sat. She got them each a glass of cabernet and joined him on the sofa. He raised his wineglass. "To us."

It was, at that moment, not the best thing he might have said. She didn't mean to look stricken, but she must have.

Without taking a sip, he set his glass on the old leather trunk that served as her coffee table and asked, too quietly, "Okay. What the hell is going on?"

She didn't know where—or how—to begin, so she knocked back a big gulp of wine. A little false courage, she decided, wouldn't hurt.

"Megan. Damn it. Talk to me...."

Her silly mouth was trembling. She pressed her lips together to make the trembling stop. "I...had lunch with your mother today."

He swore under his breath. "You what?"

"Vanessa showed up at my office. She wanted to take me to lunch."

"And you went?" He swore again. "Megan, I told you to stay away from her."

"Greg. She's your *mother.*"

"Yeah, she is. Technically. Her blood runs in my veins. But that's it. An accident of birth. In the ways that count, she's never been any kind of real mother to me. I keep as far away from her as possible as much of the time as I can. She's not a nice person, Megan. She's a self-absorbed, small-minded snob. And I'm guessing, from the brokenhearted look on your face, that today she took the gloves off and showed you what a complete bitch she can be."

Megan swallowed fiercely to keep the tears at bay. "She, um, she…said she wanted me out of your life. She said I had no…no background. That I was a nobody, a dumpy little businessperson who didn't belong in your world. She said that she could deal with you going back to Carly. Or getting together with a woman more, um, worthy of you. But what she couldn't take was your being with me. She said I would never be accepted by your family, and she thought I would be better off to just walk away now…."

Greg said yet another very bad word. "I'll talk to her. She'll apologize. I'll see to it."

"I, um…" Megan's eyes burned with the tears she was trying so hard not to shed. She pressed her fingers to her eyelids, in a futile attempt to cool the burn.

Greg took her wrists and gently pulled her hands away. "Look at me."

She made herself do it. "Oh, Greg…." He tried to gather her to him. But she resisted, pulling back, tugging on her wrists until he finally let her go. "There's more," she told him bleakly.

His big shoulders slumped. "God. I'm so damn sorry."

"It's not your fault, truly. I know it's not. Not in the least…."

"Just tell me, okay? What else?"

"Well, you, um, you know Marti, next door?"

He frowned. "Marti Vincente? Of course. What about her?"

"She was out on her lawn, this morning when you dropped me off. Remember?"

"Yeah. I guess. Vaguely…"

"She, well, she looked at me strangely."

He scowled. "Strangely? What the hell does that mean?"

"She just…she barely waved. She didn't smile. So I went over there. I asked her, you know, what was up? She told me that there's a rumor going around that you and I…a rumor that we were lovers before you and Carly broke up."

"But…that's crap."

"I know. And now Marti knows. She promised she'd start setting people straight about it. But Greg, it's all over town, that I broke up your marriage, that you and Carly would still be together if it wasn't for me."

He was shaking his head. "But it's just garbage. It's not true. Ignore it."

"It's not that easy for me, to ignore it. I…I like things kind of…low-key, you know, in my private life? I'm not used to having everybody gossiping about me. It…it doesn't work for me."

He sat very still. His eyes had gone flat. "Are you trying to tell me something, Megan? If you are, I think you should go ahead and get to the point."

Now was the time. She *had* to explain it to him, to make him understand. The problem was, it wasn't coming out the way she had planned it. "I just think, well, that this has all happened really fast, hasn't it, between you and me? Maybe a little too fast, you know?"

His face was expressionless. "No, Megan. I don't know."

She fumbled along. "I, um, well, and now you're moving to Rosewood and—"

He cut her off, coldly. "Let me get this right. What you're really saying is that you don't want me to move to Rosewood."

"No. No, I didn't say…well, yes. I mean, I could come and be with you, in the city. We could still be together…."

"Where no one in town would see us, you mean?"

Miserably, she stared at him. What could she say? He had it right—only it sounded so awful. So small-minded, didn't it? "I…"

"That *is* what you mean, isn't it?"

She gulped. And she nodded.

He said, "You're not chasing me out of Rosewood, Megan. Carly already did that once. I'm not letting it happen to me again."

"Oh!" Megan put her hand to her throat and swallowed again, hard. "Oh, of course I don't want to chase you out of town."

"You just don't want to *be* with me here, right?"

"I just…I don't know if I can handle it. All the neighbors hating me. Your own *mother* hating me. It's all just too ugly and, well, I was only thinking that if we were to sort of cool it for a while, let everybody find something else to talk about for a change, wait until Carly maybe meets someone else or something, then…" Megan didn't know how to go on. And she couldn't. Not with him looking at her as if she was someone he didn't like much and didn't know at all. Not with him angrily shaking his head.

"No," he said, and he stood.

"Oh, Greg…."

"Don't." The word was heavy with disgust. "Okay? Just don't. The deal is this. I'm so far gone on you I can't see straight. And you know what? I've always wanted what I have with you. But I didn't know the downside of it, of feeling like this. Not until the past few days, when you've been pulling away from me. It hurts. It hurts like hell. There's only one woman—you, Megan. And when you turn on me, it cuts like the sharpest knife."

She let out a cry. "Oh, no. Greg. I don't mean to—"

"But you are. You're messing with me."

"No—"

"Yeah. And I can't deal with it. I won't stand for it. Yeah, I know I said we could take it slow. I was wrong. I don't want to take it slow. I want to go for this thing with you one hundred percent. But if you think you can waffle on me and see me now and then, meet me in the city where nobody knows us…uh-uh. No way. Now and then and on-again, off-again is not what I want with you."

Why wouldn't he see? "You just don't understand. In my personal life, I need to, um, fit in. To get along with everyone. I have all the stress I can deal with already, at work. I can't take it at home, too…."

He backed up. He was shaking his head again. "I don't believe you just said that. I don't even know you when you talk like that. You're braver than that. *Better* than that."

She hung her head. Her throat had clutched up again. She whispered through the tightness. "Well, no. Not really. I'm not…"

There was a silence between them. Awful. Endless.

Finally, he said in a hollow voice, "Look at you. You're…Carly all over again, aren't you? It's all completely different. And yet it's exactly the same. Carly had secrets that kept her from being happy and really alive. And you, Megan? Brave, bold, beautiful Megan. You've got a cowardly side, a side that has you skulking away to hide in a corner when things get rough."

She made herself face him. It hurt just to look at him. She felt so…ashamed. She should say something, argue, tell him he had it all wrong.

But he didn't have it wrong. He had it horribly right.

He said, "Okay. I get it. I hear what you're telling me. This isn't going to work." He was at the door in three long strides. Softly, he told her, "Megan. Goodbye."

The hot tears started to well over. She shut her eyes, dashed those tears away.

When she looked again, he was gone.

Chapter Sixteen

It shouldn't have been that bad, should it? Shouldn't have been so *hard*.

But it was. The days went by: Saturday, Sunday, Monday. Megan went to work. She came home. She watched the kids. She went back to work in the evening. She and her team were making miracles with the Banning's account, getting raves from the Banning's executives. Gregory, Sr., liked where this was going and he made a point of telling Megan so.

Greg, however, was silent on the subject; he didn't call, e-mail or instant-message. Tuesday, one of the vice presidents on the project told her that Greg had turned the redesign over to him. Megan forced a smile and said she was sure that they would work together beautifully.

Marti heard that Greg *had* moved into the house on Sycamore Street. Irene Dare told her when Marti dropped in at Rosewood Market for a loaf of bread and a gallon of milk.

"You can bet I gave that woman a good talking-to," said Marti. "Megan, dear. Are you…all right?"

"Fine," she lied.

So Greg was in Rosewood now. He lived five blocks away—and it might as well have been five thousand miles. Lord, how Megan missed him. He was the ache in her heart, the empty place inside her, the space full of nothing that such a short time ago had been filled with light and joy, with heat and passion.

With love.

Yes. She knew it now—now that she had lost him: she loved him.

But she was a coward and he wanted— *demanded*—someone brave. Every night, she'd go home to her apartment and sit at the table and stare at the flowers he had given her that last day. They were dying now, drooping on their stems, the petals curling, turning brown, looking so sad, so far past their prime. Still, somehow, she couldn't bring herself to throw them away.

Wednesday afternoon, while she was with the kids, the doorbell rang.

Her heart raced. *Greg?* Could it be? Was it possible?

But when she pulled back the door, she found Vanessa Banning standing there. She looked Greg's mother square in the eye. "Vanessa. I don't have a thing to say to you and I'm not going to ask what you're doing here, so just head on back to the Hamptons and leave me alone." She started to shut the door in the woman's face.

But Vanessa said, "Please. I came to apologize for my behavior last week."

"Apology accepted." Again, she tried to shut the door.

"Please," Vanessa said again.

Megan peered closer at Greg's mother. The woman really did look kind of…distressed. Odd. To imagine someone like Vanessa Banning having actual emotions.

Mentally calling herself a hundred kinds of hopeless wimp, Megan gave in and let her in. The kids were in the kitchen, so Megan led Greg's mother to the living room. She gestured at a chair and took the couch for herself. "Okay," she said with mock cheer. "Go ahead. Get it over with."

Vanessa sat ramrod straight. "My son has cut me out of his life. He has told me that if I ever wish him to speak to me again, I must properly make amends for the things I said to you last Thursday. I refused. Then, yesterday, my husband came to me. Evidently, my son had talked to Gregory. Now I find my husband is making ultimatums, as well. Gregory says I have behaved very badly. He *likes* you— *admires* you, he tells me. And he will not be speaking to me, either, until I manage to make amends to you. So that's why I've come. To apologize."

"Oh," said Megan, for lack of anything more imaginative.

Vanessa tightly cleared her throat. "Tell me. What do you want me to do? How can I show my…regrets?"

Megan sighed. "Look. It doesn't matter. You've gotten your way. Greg and I broke up."

Vanessa actually blinked. "You've laid down a condition, is that it? I must apologize, or you won't take him back?"

"No condition. He broke up with me, more or less. At least, he was the one to walk out the door."

"But I don't understand. If you're no longer together, what does it matter to him if I apologize to you or not?"

Megan almost smiled. "Of course you don't understand." Funny how, now she'd lost Greg for being a coward, she was finding it a lot easier to speak up to his terrible mother. To be, at least right now, a certain kind of brave. "Your son's a wonderful man. He knows that you hurt me. He wants to be sure *I* know you're sorry."

"Well. All right, then. As I said at the door, I'm sorry."

For the first time since Greg had left her, Megan laughed. "No, you're not. But it's okay. Tell Greg you've been here and I accepted your apology. He can call me to confirm it if he doesn't believe you."

Could she bear it, if he did call? Could she keep from breaking down at the sound of his voice?

Vanessa pressed her sculpted lips together. "Well. If you're sure…"

"I am. That should solve your problem." Megan rose. "And now, I really do have to get back to the kitchen. The kids are having macaroni and cheese and if I don't hurry, there'll be none left for me. We fat girls, we really need our mac and cheese."

Vanessa flinched. "I'm sorry for that, too, for calling you fat."

Megan nodded in acknowledgment. Vanessa stood and brushed out her skirt, as if it had wrinkled, which it had not. "All right then. Thank you." She held out her hand.

Megan didn't take it. She only nodded again and gestured toward the door.

At six, with Angela home, Megan went back to Poughkeepsie.

When she returned for the night, she found her sister standing out on the front step, in the dark. Ange signaled her over. Megan nodded to let her know she'd be there.

When Megan came in from the breezeway, the kitchen smelled of something good. "Umm. Hot cocoa? In July?"

Angela chuckled. "You know you love my hot chocolate." She poured them each a mugful and they sat at the island.

"The best," Megan said, after that first delicious,

comforting sip. "And what did you need to talk about?"

Angela wrapped her hands around her mug and looked down into it, as if the answers to the basic universal questions were held in the chocolaty depths. "I'm not the one who needs to talk."

Megan sipped again before admitting, "Greg, you mean?"

Angela nodded. "Marti tells me a certain amazingly chic older woman dropped by today."

"Greg's mother." Megan shrugged. She'd already told Angela all about the lunch from hell the previous Thursday. "Vanessa came to apologize for the things she said last week. Greg made her do it. Apparently, Gregory, Sr., backed him up."

"So the woman really is sorry?"

"Doubtful. But I have to confess, sometimes it's nice to make a really awful person crawl."

The sisters looked at each other. They both giggled at the same time.

Then Angela said softly, "You miss him really bad. Don't you?"

Megan's throat did that clutching thing again. She gulped—and nodded. "But he wants—and deserves—someone braver than me. Someone who can stand tall and proud when the rumors start flying. Someone who doesn't mind being the talk of the neighborhood...."

"So." Ange sipped more cocoa. "Be that someone."

Megan blew out a frustrated breath. "Oh, yeah. Great idea. Piece of cake...."

"I'm serious. I mean it. You're brave. You just need to…have a little faith in yourself. To give yourself a chance to be your *whole* self. To quit telling yourself that you can only be strong and forceful at work, that somehow, if you stand up for yourself at home, you won't *have* a home anymore."

Out of nowhere, Megan felt the tears welling. They welled and they slid down her cheeks. "I *am* doing that, aren't I?" When her sister nodded, she said, "I didn't realize it, until just now, hearing you say it out loud…."

"And now that you realize it, I think you should stop."

"How…did you know?"

Angela's smile was infinitely loving—and so very wise. "You told me. Don't you remember? About a year after Mom and Dad adopted you, before the divorce? You said that you'd learned to be quiet, not to argue, ever. To do whatever people wanted you to do— to *be* what they wanted you to be. Because then, maybe, the next family wouldn't send you away again…."

"Oh, God…" The tears kept on falling. They dripped down her cheeks and off her chin. Ange got her a tissue and waited until she blew her nose and wiped up the flood a little.

Then her sister said, "We didn't send you away. *I* would never send you away. You're my sis. You're my kids' precious aunt Megan. You're no lost little orphan. Not anymore. You *have* a family and you always will. Me and Anthony and Olivia and Michael—we'll stick by you no matter what anyone says. Ever. Going along and fitting in might have worked for you once. But Meg—that was then. Now, you've got true love at stake. You've got to follow your heart where it leads you. You've got to stand up and be brave."

"Oh, I don't know…."

"I know you can do it," Angela said. "I know you *will*."

Chapter Seventeen

After her late-night talk with Angela, Megan began to see that it was time, at last, for her to be brave.

But she didn't feel all that brave. Not brave enough to call Greg and tell him how wrong she'd been. Not brave enough to pick up the damn phone.

Thursday went by and she took no action. Friday, too.

Saturday, for once, she didn't go to Poughkeepsie. She'd been working like a demon since Greg left her, trying not to think of him, trying not to *yearn* for him. As a result, she was about as caught up at Design Solutions as she'd ever been.

So she stayed home and cleaned her apartment. She even made herself throw out the dead bouquet

Greg had given her. She saw now that she couldn't go on clinging to a bunch of dead flowers as if they signified some kind of hope. If she wanted hope, she would have to get out there and make it happen.

The cupboards, as the old rhyme went, were bare. Though she took most of her meals with the family, she did like to keep the basics on hand at her place.

She sat down and made herself a list. Then she grabbed her purse and headed for Rosewood Market, where she strolled up and down the wide aisles, piling stuff she didn't really need into her cart, humming to herself, even grinning a little when the demonstration lady over in the produce section made a joke into her microphone that could be heard throughout the store.

Really, a Saturday off was a great thing. A day just for herself. A day to…

The random thought fled her mind half-finished. She stifled a gasp. There, right ahead of her, coming toward her in the cereal aisle, pushing a half-full cart of his own, was Greg.

Greg.

Oh, God. Her mouth went dry as a cotton swab. She licked her lips. Nodded.

He nodded back and walked on by.

Megan stared straight ahead. She forgot all about the Pop-Tarts and the Cheerios she was supposed to get in that aisle. She just put one foot in front of the other, pushing her cart blindly ahead of her, until she'd turned the corner into spices and baking goods.

About then, she shook herself.

Oh, just look at her!

Still a coward, still the same. Still a gutless, spineless, mousy little wimp. She'd walked right by him without saying a word.

What was her problem? Would she ever learn?

With a sharp cry, she abandoned her cart and raced back to cereal.

He was gone. She looked down the aisle, all the way to the end. Other shoppers stared at her. She ignored them. She whispered, miserably, "Greg. Oh, Greg..."

She caught herself. Whispering his name when he was already gone wasn't going to do her a damn bit of good.

She took off, around to the bread aisle: not there. Back to cereal; still no sign of him. To spices and baking goods: no Greg. She ran from aisle to aisle— soup to pasta to canned vegetables to coffee and condiments...

But it was no good. She couldn't find him. She'd missed her chance. Her shoulders started to slump.

And she caught herself. No! No, she hadn't missed him. Not yet. He had to be here somewhere. He couldn't have gone through the checkout line that fast.

He *had* to be here in the market somewhere....

She raced to produce. Her hungry gaze scanned the big floor bins of potatoes and onions, garlic and acorn squash. The demonstration lady stood at her microphone, cracking cooking jokes and chopping up cabbage.

And wouldn't you know it? Near the far wall, by the display of romaine and arugula, Rhonda Johnson and Irene Dare stood huddled together, staring Megan's way.

Megan refused to let them intimidate her. She looked right at them, right into their narrowed, judgmental eyes—and realized that, for the first time in her life, she didn't give a damn what they thought. Or what they said.

Because Angela had got it right. Megan Schumacher was not the skulking, scared little orphan anymore. She had people who loved her, people who would stick by her no matter what the neighbors said. By God, she was ready, at last, to stand tall and proud, to declare her love for Greg Banning loud and clear, and to hell with anyone who didn't approve.

But...

How to tell Greg she loved him, when he was nowhere in sight?

Megan's searching gaze swung toward the demonstration lady again, with her neatly curled gray hair, her half-shredded cabbage and her big, sharp knife. The woman winked at her over the rims of her glasses. "Cut it good and fine, folks. That's the secret to a great slaw." The words echoed through the store.

And all at once, Megan knew what to do.

She moved fast, before she could lose her nerve. She marched right up to the demonstration table and reached for the microphone stand, twisting it so the mike was turned her way.

"Miss?" The demonstration lady frowned, puzzled, and stopped chopping.

Megan tried not to look at that big chopping knife. "Please. I need this microphone. Just for a minute." The device picked up her voice. She heard her own words as they were broadcast through the whole market.

The demonstration lady tried to protest. "But this is not—"

"I promise," Megan interrupted. "I'll make it quick." She dragged in a big breath and spoke right into the mike. "Could I, um, have your attention please?" It came out crystal clear—and very loud.

All eyes in produce turned Megan's way. Irene and Rhonda both looked stunned. Struck speechless, for once in their mean little lives.

"Greg?" Megan said, good and strong. "Greg, if you're still in this store, it's me, Megan. Greg. And, er, everyone…" She stared straight at the two women standing slack-jawed over by the lettuce. "I have been a liar in the neighborhood. And no, it's not what you're all thinking. I was never seeing Greg Banning when he and Carly were still married. But I have been pretending to be someone I'm not anymore. And by that I mean, a doormat, a get-along kind of girl. An orphan with no one to stand up for her. A lost child who begs for a little kindness and understanding. Uh-uh. I'm not begging anymore. I haven't done anything wrong. And, Greg, from now on, whether you come over here to produce and get me or not, I'm keeping my head up and my shoulders back and…and I will be loving you, Greg Banning. No matter what anyone thinks or what anyone says. Because I, um—"

"Megan." His deep, beloved voice came from behind her.

She let out a sharp cry and whipped her head around. And there he was. Looking at her as if she was the only one in the produce section. The only one in the world. "Oh, Greg…"

"Give the woman back her microphone."

"Um. Yeah. Sure…" Megan pushed the mike back around toward the demonstration lady. "Here you go."

She chuckled, a wry sound heard throughout the store. "Well. After that, my coleslaw recipe might not seem too exciting. But we all need our fiber. So I'll just continue where I left off…."

Greg had Megan's hand. He gave a tug and she was plastered up against his broad chest. She clutched the collar of his polo shirt and looked up into those wonderful, velvet-brown eyes and suddenly, the world flew away. The demonstration lady droned on and Rhonda and Irene—and probably everyone else in produce—stared. But Megan couldn't have cared less. She had eyes only for the wonderful man who held her in his arms.

"I'm so sorry," she said. "That I wasn't...brave enough."

He touched her cheek. "I'm sorry, too. I should have been more patient. I know that. I should have given you time to find your way...."

She was shaking her head at him. "Oh, but you couldn't. I see that now. You've been patient all your life, haven't you? With your parents. With Carly. You've been waiting, I know it. For the woman you wouldn't have to be patient with. That woman was me, wasn't it?" He nodded. She added, "But then, I let you down...."

He gave her that half-smile she'd missed so much. "Funny. I don't feel the least let down now."

She said, "Greg Banning, I love you. I love you so much."

And he said, "As I love you." And then he scooped her high into his arms and carried her out of there, past the bins of fruit and the salad dressing display, through the bakery section, past the checkout stands and straight toward the automatic doors.

Megan wrapped her arms around his neck and beamed a proud smile at all the staring shoppers, as Greg carried her out the sliding glass doors into the blinding brightness of that sunny afternoon.

He paused at the edge of the parking lot. "Where to?" he asked.

And so she told him, firm and clear, loudly enough that anyone could hear, "It doesn't matter. Anywhere. Just as long as I'm with you."

* * * * *

*Beautiful Carly Alderson has been having a
difficult time getting over her ex-husband.
Then she meets contractor Bo Conway....
Don't miss
THE PERFECT WIFE
by reader favorite Judy Duarte
The next installment of the new
Special Edition continuity
TALK OF THE NEIGHBORHOOD
On sale August 2006,
wherever Silhouette books are sold.*

Join Sheri WhiteFeather in The Trueno Brides!

Don't miss the first book in the trilogy:

EXPECTING THUNDER'S BABY

Sheri WhiteFeather
(SD #1742)

Carrie Lipton had given Thunder Trueno her heart. But their marriage fell apart. Years later Thunder was back. A reckless night of passion gave them a second chance for a family, but would their past stand in the way of their future?

On sale August 2006 from Silhouette Desire!

Make sure to read the next installments in this captivating trilogy by Sheri WhiteFeather:

MARRIAGE OF REVENGE,
on sale September 2006

THE MORNING-AFTER PROPOSAL,
on sale October 2006!

Available wherever books are sold,
including most bookstores, supermarkets,
discount stores and drugstores.

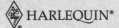

HARLEQUIN®

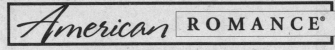

IS PROUD TO PRESENT A GUEST APPEARANCE BY

QUILL
BOOK
AWARD
WINNING
AUTHOR

NEW YORK TIMES bestselling author
DEBBIE MACOMBER

The Wyoming Kid

The story of an ex–rodeo cowboy,
a schoolteacher and their journey to the altar.

"Best-selling Macomber, with more than
100 romances and women's fiction titles
to her credit, sure has a way of pleasing readers."
—*Booklist* on *Between Friends*

**The Wyoming Kid is available from
Harlequin American Romance in July 2006.**

www.eHarlequin.com   HARDMJUL

If you enjoyed what you just read,
then we've got an offer you can't resist!

Take 2 bestselling
love stories FREE!
Plus get a FREE surprise gift!

Stability is highly overrated....

Dana Logan's world had always revolved around her children. Now they're all grown up and don't seem to need anything she's able to give them. Struggling to find her new identity, Dana realizes that it's about time for her to get "off her rocker" and begin a new life!

Off Her Rocker

by Jennifer Archer

HN53

Available August 2006
TheNextNovel.com

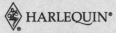

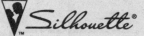

COMING NEXT MONTH

#1771 BACK IN THE BACHELOR'S ARMS—Victoria Pade
Northbridge Nuptials
Years ago, when Chloe Carmichael was pregnant by high school
sweetheart Reid Walker, her meddling parents sent her out of town and
told Reid she'd lost the baby. Now Chloe was back to sell her parents'
old house—and *Dr.* Reid Walker was the buyer. Soon he discovered the
child he never knew…and rediscovered the woman he'd never forgotten.

#1772 FINDING NICK—Janis Reams Hudson
Tribute, Texas
Shannon Malloy's book about 9/11 heroes was almost done—but when
she tracked her last interview subject, injured New York firefighter
Nick Carlucci, to Tribute, Texas, he wasn't talking. While Nick denied
Shannon access to his story, he couldn't deny her access to his heart—
especially when he realized their shared connection to the tragedy….

#1773 THE PERFECT WIFE—Judy Duarte
Talk of the Neighborhood
Rich, thin Carly Anderson had a fairy-tale life…until her husband left
her for her friend down the street. Carly became reclusive—maybe even
chubby!—but when worried neighbors coaxed her out to the local pool,
she was pleasantly surprised to meet carpenter Bo Conway. Would this
down-to-earth man help Carly get to *happily ever after* after all?

#1774 OUTBACK BABY—Lilian Darcy
Wanted: Outback Wives
City girl Shay Russell had come to the Australian Outback in flood
season to rethink her values. And when she dropped into cattleman Dusty
Tanner's well-ordered life after a helicopter crash, two worlds literally
collided. Soon, not only the waters, but the passions, were running high
on the Outback….until Shay told Dusty she was pregnant.

#1775 THE PRODIGAL M.D. RETURNS—Marie Ferrarella
The Alaskans
Things really heated up in Hades, Alaska, when skirt-chasing
Ben Kerrigan came back to town. But after leaving Heather Ryan
Kendall at the altar seven years ago, Dr. Ben was a reformed man.
Soon Ben was back paying Heather personal house calls…but recently
widowed Heather and her six-year-old daughter had a surprise for the
prodigal M.D.

#1776 JESSIE'S CHILD—Lois Faye Dyer
The McClouds of Montana
Even a decades-old family feud couldn't stop Jessie McCloud and Zack
Kerrigan from sharing a night of passion—just one night. But four years
later, when Zack returned from military duty overseas, he discovered
that *just one night* had had lifelong consequences. Could Jessie and
Zack overcome dueling family traditions to raise their son…together?